ORIGIN OF EXILES
FABLES OF TARLATAN
BOOK I

SAMANTHA DEPERGOLA

To all those who felt as though the world was crushing down on them, and they learned how to lift it.

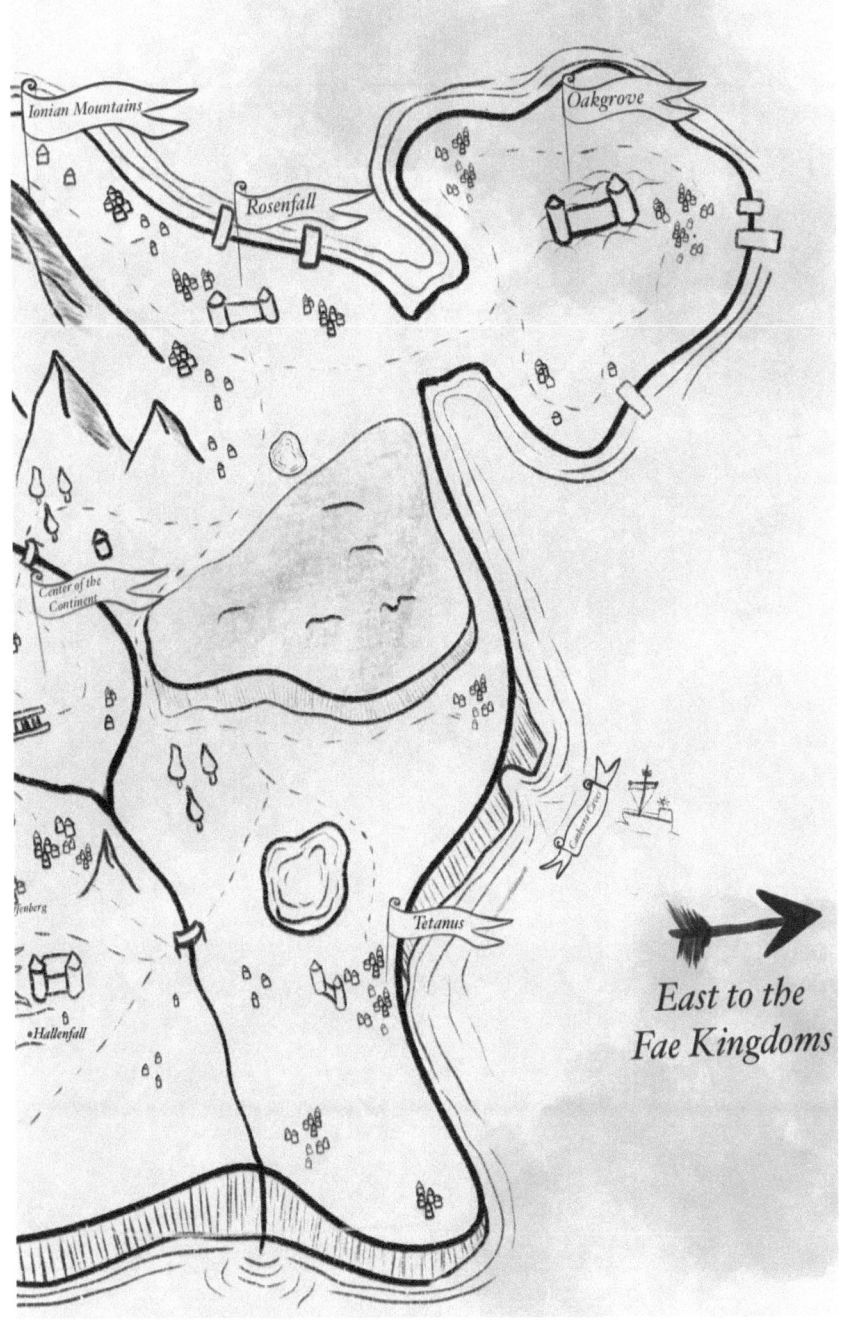

CONTENTS

CHAPTER 1

THE HEART OF THE DRAGON

'LEGEND HAS IT, FORTY YEARS AGO, A DRAGON SACRIFICED ITS gold for a child. Forty years ago, legend says, it was discovered a dragon had a heart.

A hot breath filled the cave. Soft snoring could be heard for miles, but it didn't deter the little feet from pitter pattering into the cave. Trepidation filled every step but going back was a far worse fate than entering.

They had no choice but to face the behemoth before them- a red dragon taller than anything they had ever seen before, even lying down. Small spurts of fire popped out with each snore.

The little feet pitter pattered close, getting slower with each step until it had reached the dragon. It was almost too hot if they stood in front of the nose- they would have to stand to the side, just below the eye.

A tiny finger reached out, poking a scale on the snout of the dragon. Before they could even consider running away as fast as their little legs could take them, an eyelid snapped open, and a golden eye peered below.

"Interesting..." The words murmured throughout the room, echoing off the walls.

The dragon shifted its head, lifting it off the ground to get a better view.

A child, no more than five years old stood in a ripped tunic, had bare feet, and something that looked like it was once a pair of pants. The dragon almost wept fiery tears at the child. The child was covered in dirt with its long, tangled hair looking closer to a bird's nest. But the child wasn't trembling or crying- no, those clear tracks down the child's cheeks were dry and from tears before he had stumbled upon this cave.

Fire rumbled in the dragon's chest. He had been half asleep, listening to those feet enter his cave. He had even gone as far as to snore to lure in unwitting knights or robbers who thought they had a chance against him. Instead, those knights and robbers would have ended up being an easy meal.

"Do you know who I am, child?" The dragon spoke, pulling his mind from his slumber. The child shook its head, playing with the fraying ends of the tunic.

What circumstances had this child come from where they weren't even scared of the dragon? Had the child not heard tales of Thermaxas, the red dragon that haunted the forests of Nazare?

The dragon willed whatever fire was brewing to cool down, so as to not scare the child. "Child, what do you seek?" His words were soft, and he set his head against the cool floor of the cave- if that made him seem any smaller, any more approachable, he had no idea.

"I was scared. My momma... Papa was hitting her. He was hitting me before. Momma told me to run as fast and as far as I could. I remembered the stories my momma would tell me about a dragon coming to destroy our house. I thought maybe you could help scare Papa from hitting Momma." The child spoke slowly, each word a spear to the dragon's heart. Whatever control the dragon had over its fire wouldn't last much longer. The child plopped onto the ground, tears threatening to spill over.

The dragon gently nuzzled the child, careful not to knock it over. Trying to distract himself from the fact that the child had thought its father was more dangerous than a dragon.

"Where does your Papa and Momma live, child?" The dragon hoped that this child, although little, was taught enough to know where he had lived. The child spoke well enough that he must have come from a family with money.

The child bowed its head a little more, its bottom lip quivering. The dragon nuzzled it a little more before he felt cool tears drip onto his scales. They ran down the dragon's muzzle until they were nothing more.

"Child, do you want my help? I cannot give it to you if you do not know where you are from…" The dragon attempted to soften his voice. As if the voice was not coming out of a fire breathing beast with impenetrable scales and near impenetrable wings.

The child backed away a little, playing with the hem of its tunic. "My momma always called it hell. I think my Papa called it…" The child paused, scrunching its nose. "Gruff… Gruffen…" The dragon's fire roared in his chest.

"Gruffenberg?" Somehow, despite the anger flowing through his veins, his voice stayed soft. The child nodded. "Can you climb up my wing onto my back? If you sit in between the spikes and hold onto one, you will not fall. Whatever happens, do not leave my back when we get there."

He felt small, nimble, unsure feet climb up its wing. They pressed into one spot, sending tickles down the dragon's spine. He had to suppress every urge to stretch his wing out to avoid sending the child flying off. He rolled his head, trying to remember *why that village had sounded so familiar.* But he couldn't think past the anger, and once the child was seated, he walked out of his cave.

The dragon turned his head back just a little, eyeing the sparkles of gold that could still be seen at the entrance. They whispered to him, those sparkles. Trying to entice him back to protect them. But the shaking of the child that sat upon his back was enough to ignore the whispers and fly off to Gruffenberg.

The entire flight there, he felt the child trembling against his back, clutching onto the spikes on his back for dear life. The dragon found himself trying to control his anger so he would not burn down the village just as he arrived. So, he let the wind flow off his scales, cooling the fire building in his chest. Gruffenberg was lucky he was not a black dragon... A black dragon was so deadly they would have felt its heat from miles away.

And as he flew in closer, circling overhead, he realized why Gruffenberg was so familiar.

Gruffenberg was a small town set beyond a forest, with fields just tilled. They raised cows in a pasture just beyond the village. For a small town in Statium away from the hectic capital of Hallenfall, it was luxurious. The town center was a courtyard with a fountain that glittered and there was a tavern on every street corner. The streets were kept clean, with waste being dumped in a tunnel that led to a river downstream.

Thermaxas had discovered long ago that all that glittered was not often gold.

Townsfolk came flying out of their homes, pitchforks and spears clutched in their hands. He blinked down his third eyelid, protecting his eyes from any projectiles. The red dragon let loose a roar, letting the townsfolk know who had come to demand payment.

They would regret the day this child had come pitter pattering into his cave.

He swooped in low and landed in the town common, nearly taking up the entire space. Townsfolk were pressed against buildings, pointing their dull spears and pitchforks out towards him.

The red dragon snorted in amusement. "I've come for the mother of this child. Deliver her to me, and no harm will come to this village today."

A murmur shuttered through the crowd before a startled cry rose out. A woman ran forward, covered in bruises and dirt. There, not too far behind her, was a man that followed her. He grabbed onto her shift and pulled her back. She fell to the ground, stifling the grunt of pain that followed.

The child on his back clutched the spike harder. "Momma!"

That cry sent embers flying out of his nose.

"Jonathon! Baby!" Her cries flooded the common, her begging for her child nearly unbearable. The child stayed upon his back.

The man grabbed her shift and pulled her roughly back again as she stood. "Stay down, woman. I will deal with my son. This is the business of men." He sneered at her, spitting at her feet.

More embers flew from his nose. The child whimpered on his back but did not dare slide off.

The dragon stepped forward, taking one claw and pushing the pitchforks and spears away. One of the men even stepped forward with his spear and Thermaxas growled. "That would most certainly not be in your best interest."

The child's father stepped forward, staring the dragon down.

Interesting reaction, the dragon thought.

"You will give me my child back you beast. You took our gold, burned our crops, and have kept traders away with your snoring. The few that dare travel past your cave to get to

Gruffenberg speak of the untold horrors they had to face." The man was shouting, rousing the townsfolk behind him. "Come here, Jonathon. You know better to run."

The child shook violently, sliding down the dragons back. The dragon heard the child's little feet hit the ground. In an instant, a wing flew out and pushed the child back towards the dragon's side.

"You townsfolk call me a beast? You would watch this monster beat his wife and child while doing nothing to stop him. The crimes you accuse me of?" The dragon scoffed. "I took your gold because you offered it to me. *'Keeping the beast at bay'* if I recall correctly. I burned your crops because they were full of pestilence and had you eaten them, you would have fallen deathly ill. No traders have faced horrors from me. In fact, several do business with me. They stay away from your town at their own expense."

Another man spoke up. "It is not our business what a man does with his property. You have no business here, beast. Leave our town be. You have caused enough trouble already." The dragon could have laughed. That fire stirred deep in his belly, begging to be released.

"This child and woman are property of no man. They are their own beings. If you view them as property, you are more a beast than I." The dragon was silent. "I do have a proposition for you. I will give you all the gold in my cave in exchange for all of the women and children."

The townsfolk that had been jeering went silent.

"All... All of your hoard?" The men salivated. He could smell their excitement. The dragon nodded. "It is a deal. You will bring the gold to us and then we will give you our women and children."

"No. A dragon can never break his word- I give you my word that I will bring you all the gold in my hoard, should you let me take the women and children now- unharmed, and alive."

Silence. For only a millisecond.

"Take them. We don't want them. We will buy other whores to warm our beds and give us heirs." The father's child grabbed the woman by the shift and practically threw her at the dragon, who snarled in warning.

For three days, the women, children, and dragon wandered back. The men at the village had given him a week to get the gold back to them. They wandered through the forest, most of the women staying as far away from him as possible. The child, Jonathon, had slept at his side every night.

Jonathon's mother eventually gave in that first night, not baring to be far from her child. She eventually thanked him for his sacrifice and fell asleep crying like most nights. The dragon noticed that most women fell asleep crying and each time he heard those sobs, the fire within him stirred. Some women would awake from dreams that seemed more like nightmares and not go back to sleep.

Thermaxas had to wonder if some women thought him more a monster than the men he had rescued them from.

When the dragon had brought the women and children to his cave, he did not bring them inside. He did not want them to feel trapped or like property.

"Women, children... You are free to go wherever you wish. I have a second hoard of gold in a mountain in the north that I will retrieve after I bring the gold back to the men. I will distribute it evenly across you all so that you may live in comfort for the rest of your days. The only request I make is that you not return to Gruffenberg." He tried to seem as non-threatening as possible but knew the women would be hesitant no matter how much he curled in on himself.

One woman stepped forward. "Why should we believe you? You have stolen us from our men!"

Another stepped forward, staring in disbelief at that woman. "Our men just sold us like cattle! This dragon at least gives us an attempt at another life. I know the bruises and cuts that you hide underneath your kirtle, Helen." Helen, despite the rage on her face, stepped back. The woman looked towards the dragon. "Thank you for your kindness. Do not expect a thank you from the rest of the women. They have been beaten into submission for their entire life and know little else."

He knew as much- he had come across women in similar situations, but he had never had the opportunity to help them. It would take them time to adjust and heal.

There was fire in this woman's eyes. The dragon knew that if she was too a dragon, he would have wanted to be her mate. "I guess you do not hail from Gruffenberg?"

"No, dragon. I am Gemella of Velletia. I was sold by my parents when they lost their wealth to a man who lied through his teeth. It will take time for the women here to realize what life is like outside towns like Gruffenberg." The women had softened a little, but that fire did not go out.

The dragon nodded, looking at all the women again. "If you wish to restart your life with the gold I have promised, you will stay here until I return in a week's time. There are stores of food in the cave from a party that tried to steal from my hoard not two weeks ago that should be good. Feed your children with that. Jerky is kept there as well." The dragon turned and began to walk into his cave but heard little feet pattering after him.

Jonathon stood before him, tears in his eyes. "Please do not leave us. Who will keep us safe? What if Poppa comes back for us?" Fire stirred in the dragon's belly.

"Child, if any man returns to take you from your home, you will let them know that you have a soul tie with Thermaxas the Bloody. If they take you, I will find you, Jonathon. Call for me and I will be there, no matter how far away you might be."

With that, the dragon stalked into his cave and stared at the hoard three levels down, wondering how he was going to transport *this much gold*. He winced but took to the nearest town and found a ship for sale.

He got a good deal for the ship, ripped out the floor, and filled the entire ship with gold. When he discovered there was still some gold left over, Thermaxas was forced to buy two wagons that he would have to pull behind him.

Which would mean flying low and slow, Thermaxas thought.

Sometimes he wished he was a black dragon who did not care about the world around him.

But Thermaxas was not a black dragon, and he did care about the world around him. He would not have gotten to see the reactions from the men of Gruffenberg who witnessed Thermaxas pull two wagons into their town common, and plunk a small warship next to their dry fountain.

And those women and children back outside his cave… They would have continued to suffer in this town, being treated no better than an animal. He would not have gotten to save them from this horrific fate.

"Men, we eat and drink well tonight! Leave us be, you beast. I trust our business is over with."

And so, he was dismissed. Thermaxas did not fly far, only the next mountain over. He watched for two nights as the town was filled with merriment, women of the night coming and going. The third night left the men alone in their town, shit and trash lying in the streets. Drunk men lay on street corners, others stumbling down the alleyways, and some sleeping in the pile of gold.

Thermaxas waited patiently those three nights. He kept an eye on his gold, noting how much came and went. They spent a surprising amount in those three nights, but it did not matter. They did not make enough of a dent in the pile that sat in their town common.

Each night the fire in his soul grew hotter, until it was so hot Thermaxas was worried it might burn him from the inside out.

It was only then that Thermaxas the Bloody flew from his nest and circled the town common, letting out a mighty roar to awaken the men. They were in drunken hazes, disorientated from the three sleepless nights. Some wet themselves and hid while others attempted to run. Most of the men went to the town common though, staring up at Thermaxas.

"What is the meaning of this, beast? Our business is concluded!"

A mighty roar was the only answer Thermaxas gave. If they could only think of him as a beast... He would remind them just how kind he had been all these years. He would show them the horrors he had spared them from. The men scrambled upon the ship, trying to rush to the highest point to throw spears.

Thermaxas merely circled, drawing in more and more men, until he was confident that almost the entirety of the men were there.

It was then that Thermaxas the Bloody showed them the beast inside.

He loosed his hellfire upon the gold hoard that sat in the town center. The ship and wagons burned up almost immediately, the gold scattering across the ground. His hellfire burned so hot it was tinted blue and men screamed, trying in vain to run away.

That was only the first few seconds.

After that, the gold had melted, turning molten and rushing through the streets. It covered the pavers in gold, melting off the feet of men it was so hot. The dragon felt a thrill roll through him, seeing the gold melt through the streets and catch the men. He flew low, corralling men back into the chaos. A laugh tumbled out of his chest and for a moment, he forgot what had caused this. He flew through the town, tearing through buildings and burning town cottages.

The dragon picked up men and tore them in half as he threw them in the air.

A wicked joy kept that fire blazing hot in his chest. It had been so very, *very* long since he had razed a village to the ground.

The horrors that befell the town this fateful night took a full day to unfold. Thermaxas hunted men down who had run from the village, torturing some longer than others.

The child's father felt his full wrath as he dunked him in and out of the gold, slowly. He kept his fire low in his chest as not to kill the man too quickly.

Eventually, Thermaxas turned back to himself. By the time he finished, it had turned to day and night fell again. Quiet pride thrummed throughout his body that fourth night, and he flew to the north in satisfaction. There he filled a canvas tarp with gold to bring back to the women and children.

Seven days after he had left them, Thermaxas had returned as promised.

As he approached the entrance to clearing in front of his cave, he found about half of the women and children gone. Sadness chased that pride away, but he knew that he could do nothing more. Those women were free to go wherever they wished. They were no longer caged animals underneath the thumb of men lesser than them.

Thermaxas prayed to whatever Gods still listened that the women and children did not return to that village.

The remaining women and children cautiously approached him. Worry flickered through his chest that they might be able to scent what had occurred in Gruffenberg. But the race of man did not have the same ability of scenting as the immortals and beasts of Tarlatan had. Even if they did, the winds had long washed off whatever scent had remained of the brutal events.

"Is it okay if we stay here to establish a camp while we figure out where we will go? One of the other women knows of a town not too far from here and promises that it is not the same as Gruffenberg. It is a small fishing village near a river, do you know of it?" Jonathon's mother spoke, standing out next to Gemella.

The dragon nodded. "The men there are good. It is a rather small community. If you wish to go further, a city is about a weeks' journey from here. It is a coastal city ripe with trade and food. It has not seen war in many moons. However, no matter how long it takes, you will always be welcome to camp here. I will ensure you are safe until you decide to move on."

The women and children stayed outside his mountain for roughly two months, trying to decide where to go. Eventually the group split up, with a little under half going to that village and the rest going to the coastal city. Gemella returned to Velletia, where her parents are said to have welcomed her back with open arms. The dragon gave her a little extra gold, telling her to return wealth to her family and Velletia.

Twenty one years after the fateful day his little feet pitter-pattered into the cave of a red dragon, he had finally returned. As Jonathon grew from a child into a young man, he felt the soul tie tugging at him.

The cave was the same as he remembered it. Dimly lit the further you walked in, the floor practically shaking with the snores of the dragon.

A disgruntled voice came from deep within the cave. "Jonathon, if that is you attempting to sneak, I am incredibly disappointed."

And so, Jonathon and the dragon were reunited. It was a night full of mirth as much as it was of pain. Thermaxas learned from Jonathon that not too long after they had gone to that coastal city, his mother had taken up work at a woman's shelter. Unfortunately, as Jonathon grew older, he was not allowed to live there with his mother. The shelter apologized profusely but explained that his presence would frighten women who had been in a situation like his mother's.

Thermaxas bristled at that, but his fire burned hot as Jonathon explained he was homeless. At one point men had even tried to kidnap him, but when Jonathon was being dragged into that home, he invoked the soul tie... And the men were sent running. The dragon smiled proudly at that.

"Child... No matter how old you grow, I will always be proud of you. I have felt you through the soul tie. Your fear, your joy, your anger... I thought I felt you tug at the soul tie once. But when I felt the joy and relief that followed it, I remained knowing you were safe. How are you getting by nowadays?" Thermaxas was curled up in a corner of the cave and had lit a fire for Jonathon. They were both eating mutton that Thermaxas had caught earlier in the day.

"I am a part of a company of men and women that are traveling the country. We are warriors, farmers, priests, and teachers. For the past year, we've been assisting small villages who were hit hard by famine." Jonathon gulped. "Thermaxas... The kingdoms... Things are shifting. It feels as though a great evil is coming through."

Thermaxas bristled, lifting his head. "What do you mean?" The dragon was immortal, or as close to it as any mortal could come. He had lived for five hundred years and would live for another ten thousand more before he grew too old to continue.

Jonathon downed the rest of his ale. "People say that it didn't just stop when Luce Stellarum fell. They say that their Sentinels have been lost and will never return. Oakgrove is scrambling its armies to its borders, but people do not know why. Rosenfall's Queen still has not returned and it is said a steward rules in her place."

Thermaxas plopped his head back onto the ground, letting out a breath. Embers flew out and the fire rose higher. He had seen kingdom's rise and fall. He had seen evil. But what Jonathon was saying… Thermaxas had long felt unsettled. He had assumed his age was catching up to him already, that he would be one of those dragons who were not as long lived as the rest.

Deep down, he knew that wasn't true.

"The Sentinels… They are truly lost?" Thermaxas had remembered when they had been born. Immortal women warriors, some descended from the gods themselves. Products of the Fae and humans interbreeding.

Jonathon nodded grimly. "That's what I've heard."

"They were immortal… For them to have fallen… I suspect you are right. That is why the bond called us together. For you to warn me and… For me to explain what this soul tie is, exactly." Jonathon raised an eyebrow. "The soul tie… Binds a magical creature to a child in need. The child may or may not be magical. You have become my ward, essentially. You were fearless when you approached me, and your soul tied itself to my own because you saw past the beast within. You are still a mortal. If you possessed magical qualities, you might have been able to speak the tongue of dragons…"

Thermaxas sighed and stared Jonathon down.

"The soul tie only occurs every so often. I have never known a dragon to receive a soul tie. It is said that we are soul-less. But it seems we broke the mold." Thermaxas explained it as simply as he could. Soul ties were once things of legend, until now. The moment Thermaxas had seen Jonathon walk into his cave when he was only a child… It was unquestion-able. Thermaxas would do anything for Jonathon, even if it meant that Thermaxas would die.

"I have heard stories about soul ties. The things that magic holding mortals can do when they are soul tied to magical creatures. Does this mean evil is truly coming?" Jonathon took another bite of mutton and took a sip out of another mug of ale.

All Thermaxas could do was nod.

"Thermaxas… I know what happened to Gruffenberg." The dragon's head whipped so fast back towards Jonathon that he almost made himself dizzy.

No. Not this. Jonathon had an army behind him. Jonathon was coming to kill him.

Panic flooded the dragon. He had come to love this mortal as his own, he realized.

"When me and my mother made it to the coastal city, we told them we came from Gruffenberg. We had no idea what happened- but the people spoke of the horrors that occurred. How the men were tortured. How one man was so badly tortured he was barely recognizable, except for the scar above his right eyebrow that no one else had possessed."

Thermaxas stilled. Not even the fire in his chest dared to flare.

Gods don't let it end like this.

"No one who visited Gruffenberg dared go for that gold for fear Thermaxas the Bloody would come to do the same to their village. It is said a dragon never loses the scent of his hoard once he has touched it. That gold could be halfway around the world and you could still smell it, they said." Jonathon put his mug of ale down and stood in front of Thermaxas.

He put his head on his snout and rubbed the scales of the dragon. Relief flooded through Thermaxas. "I tried to tell them that my father deserved it. That, had it not been for you, I would have died. They didn't believe me. When those men tried to take me when I was living on the streets, and I told them about the soul tie, I pulled out a piece of your gold. It had the imprint of one of your scales on it- you must have laid on it when you were particularly hot that day. They recoiled so quickly that I thought they might begin to grovel if I didn't put the gold away."

Thermaxas blew out a breath and placed his head on the ground. Laid out his wing on the ground, careful not to knock over Jonathon's things. The young man sat on the ground and leaned against Thermaxas' snout, so close to the jagged teeth.

Jonathon had never feared Thermaxas. Why would he have come back to kill him? Thermaxas actually laughed. He had been panicking for nothing.

"Jonathon, I have lived for five hundred years. I have seen evil rise and fall. But... This will be different. I have never been so unsettled. No matter what happens, should you ever feel the least bit of fear, I will come for you. Promise me that you'll call for me."

Jonathon promised. And the next day, he left Thermaxas for his company who was staying in the nearest town. It wasn't a tearful goodbye, for Jonathon promised to meet Thermaxas on the return trip back.

Legend has it, the dragon had gone into hiding when Jonathon returned, for Thermaxas and his newly acquired gold were not there when Jonathon returned. Jonathon had felt in his soul for that tie, and sent a call down it- not for help, but one telling Thermaxas... That if he needed help. Jonathon would come find him too.'

The man went silent, smiling to himself. He took a gulp from his tankard of ale and fingered the piece of gold in his pocket.

"Mister, what happened after that?" A young girl, who was piled in amongst the other street children, raised her hand eagerly and waved it about.

The man took another drink. "Jonathon did not see Thermaxas again, but never had reason to call for him."

Another child waved their hand about. "Will Jonathon ever call for him?"

The man smiled again and shrugged his shoulders. "That is for Jonathon to answer."

The street children, thoroughly bored with that answer, got up and looked for another more interesting stranger to go bother. They ran about the streets, dodging wagons and horses.

Out of the corner of his eye, Jonathon saw a woman come up. She had auburn hair and the tipped ear of the Fae, which she attempted to hide beneath the hood of her cloak. The cloak was pinned with a clasp made of a sword and twisting vines.

"What about the Sentinels? Did they remain lost?" The man shrugged his shoulders at that, too.

"Your guess is as good as mine, Lady. I would have thought they would have returned to their Fae ancestors after Luce Stellarum fell, though. People say they're never coming back." The man stood from his stool, beginning to pack his things. Out of the corner of his eye, he watched a dagger fall out of her sleeve.

The man felt for that piece of gold again. Wondered if that good time might be now.

"We did not return to the Fae. They refused our call for aid."

Jonathon froze but gripped the piece of gold. He didn't question himself when he sent that frazzled thought down the soul tie.

Rage and comfort rippled in response.

"We, Lady?" Jonathon continued to pack his things as he watched the woman.

She nodded her head. "Yes, we. We did not return to the Fae. They betrayed us by not helping us. A few who longed to see their mothers returned, but most did not. I am a Sentinel of the Fallen Kingdom and you will bring me to Thermaxas."

"What business do you have with Thermaxas? On whose orders?" It was no point telling the Sentinel that he did not know who Thermaxas was. She already knew that he was the boy in the story and had likely been tracking him for days.

"My business is my own." She stopped circling him. She spun the dagger in her hand, staring him down.

A roar sounded in the distance. The town stopped silent. Jonathon smiled- always a grand entrance.

The Sentinel looked at him in disbelief. "You called him?"

"Thermaxas was always protective. He was probably already flying over."

The world shook with another roar. As if confirming that he had felt Jonathon's fear and would answer even if he didn't call.

The Sentinel pulled the sword from her side out and held it loosely, watching Thermaxas circle above before landing outside the city. Jonathon and the Sentinel both walked towards him, dodging people who ran away from him. Confused screams filled the city, some wondering why he wasn't attacking and others wondering if he was just waiting for them to panic more.

Thermaxas loosed a small breath of fire, rage rippling at the soul tie. "The next time you wish to see me, Sentinel, you will not use Jonathon to do so."

The Sentinel did not sheath her sword but did bow, a little. She walked up, much closer than Jonathon would have thought was wise. "Thermaxas, we have an issue. Evil is threatening Tarlatan. My sisters are rallying forces to try and protect king- doms, but we alone are not enough. We need allies."

"And why would the Sentinels want to ally with Thermaxas the Bloody?" The dragon snorted. Jonathon watched in awe as he witnessed history take place.

"Because Thermaxas, this evil is so deep rooted even you will not outlast it alone. And I think your ward was correct- you do have a heart and could not bear seeing Jonathon die. Could you imagine that feeling rippling down the soul bond?"

Thermaxas snarled. "Do not threaten my ward or you will find yourself without a head, Sentinel or not."

'Then stop being so broody and meet us in the Ionian mountains." The Sentinel sheathed her sword and pulled out an invitation. The invitation was sealed with wax and stamped with the crest of Rosenfall.

Thermaxas cocked his head and furrowed his brows. "Who is us?"

The Sentinel wore a wicked smile.

CHAPTER 2
THE CANBERRAN PIRATE LORDS

"I EXPECTED YOU WOULD BE HERE." THE VOICE WAS TOO gentle, as if it was trying not to scare off a petrified rabbit.

"Well, that's not good at all. I'll have to switch it up a bit. Can't be predictable now, can we?" She shorted, shaking her head. She sat on the bench, staring out over the ocean. Her brother was walking up behind her and sat next to her.

"What we need to do is talk about this. You haven't been yourself." She frowned. The conversation took a turn she could have spotted a mile away, but she had been praying that she could avoid it. Her brother had been trying to contact her relentlessly... At first she tried to talk to him, but he never moved to help her- just control her.

So, she eventually stopped talking about it at all.

"You know nothing about me. This needs to end. You cannot define what my habits should be by what you had once grown used to." Her words were hissed, violent- warning him that he was treading on dangerous ground. She felt her brother stiffen next to her and stand up sharply.

She was sure that in the rehearsed version in his head, she

was a sniffling sobbing mess at his feet right now. But she had been pushed too far past that point.

"Ana, you don't sleep. You don't eat. Gods damn it all, I can count on one hand alone the number of times I've seen you this week! Two months ago, I couldn't get you out of the house. Now, I can't seem to get you to return a letter. So don't you dare try to tell me I know nothing." He threw his hands up in the air, rubbing his face. "Ana, come on. My kids are worried. I don't know how much longer I can keep lying to them."

"Four months ago, our father died. Three weeks ago, we buried him ten feet underground to the sounds of war horns blaring. Two and a half weeks ago, Oakgrove's Treasury denied us compensation for the funeral affairs- something they were supposed to pay for based on the papers he signed from the war with Rosenfall. They also held a grudge against me from when I left their service to help our father. You wonder why I can't fucking sleep? I have a gods damned dog I need to keep fed. The tavern refuses to keep me scheduled because our father died- apparently, I can't be deemed stable because I've just been through a "tragic" time and they're nervous I'll steal from them. I owe the baker down the street 12 gold pieces, and yeah, in case you were wondering, I'm pretty sure I sprained my gods damned wrist. It hurts like a son of a bitch, but all I can do is grit my teeth because I can't afford a visit to the healer." Ana paused. Slowly, she stood up. Winding her arm back, she whipped the rock as far as she could, hearing the satisfying plunk as it dropped into the ocean. With a low, cynical tone, she continued. "What's even worse? The only place I have to live is our father's cottage, because I don't have to pay for it. It's just a one room cottage with a well and a fireplace. Every day I see the stains from dead deer and rabbits. I remember gutting fish and squir-rels in this exact spot when times got rough. Just me and dear old dad, because *you* abandoned us for the fancy city living. Everywhere around me are memories that haunt me every single day. And I can't get an ounce of sleep because it all keeps me up."

He was quiet. As if he wasn't expecting her to pour out her whole life story onto one plate and make him swallow the whole meal in one go.

She placed her head in her hands and rubbed her temples. This wasn't how she had wanted to spend her day. But... But this was the last place she had talked with her father. And he died on this day four months ago.

She had spent months- *months* – bartering for funeral services for her father. Analise wasn't even sure if there had been a body to bury or if they had just burned the corpse rather than wait for her to find the money. So... This was the one spot she knew a part of her father still lived on.

She was pouring her heart out to her father before her brother had interrupted. She knew the words would be carried across the wind and heard by no one. But a small part of her had hoped her father would hear, even in the afterlife.

"Ana, you know I'm a healer, I could have gotten you he-" Oh, she just laughed. Her little brother, he tried so dearly to help. To compensate for where he had greatly underestimated just how much her life had gotten twisted.

So, she stopped him. "Help? How could you have helped? Dropped off a sleeping tonic? Paid the funeral expenses? Oh, this is the real kicker- do you think you could have possibly dropped me off at the looney bin to help me sleep and, maybe, process?" Analise growled the words out, at just barely louder than a whisper.

Her brother would have never done anything other than that. He had always been blind to how her and her father had struggled. He could only focus on *him*. He could never just be there or offer help without her begging.

"Ana... I don't, I don't know how to help you other than

that." Her poor little brother was left fumbling for words. They had never clicked- always argued over how her father could have done more and didn't need to leave their burdens all on her shoulders. They had always been exact opposites, never quite being able to understand each other.

"Then why the hell are you here? So we can talk about our feelings, and pretend that you never abandoned me and Dad? So we can be a *family* again?" She was seething by now and spoke barely above a whisper. Ana stood, looking up to her little brother and staring him in the eyes. For someone who was so tall, her brother had never been able to intimidate. But her little brother, who never had an angry bone in his body, finally got frustrated. His whole face went red, and his fists curled.

Oh, she knew she was taunting him, and it was *so much fun.*

"Do not pin that shitshow on me! He is the one who abandoned this family. He is the one that brought you out here, convinced you to join the navy with him. He is the one that went on a drinking binge when Mom died! Do not blame that drunken bastard's antics on me." Screaming louder and louder as he talked, her brother backed further away- and for the first time in her life, she thought he might hit her. His knuckles were white as he clenched his fists. And all she could do was breathe in and out, slowly.

And right when her brother unclenched his fists a second later, she curled up her own and wound her arm back, only to shove it in his face as hard as she could.

He staggered back, hunched over, and was breathing heavily. Blood dripped slowly, like a leaky tap. Ana couldn't see the damage she had done, but from his reaction, she guessed that his nose had been broken.

"Crazy fucking bitch!" Her throat closed. Her brother's voice cracked. Ana's hands began to shake. He cupped his face, as he breathed heavily through the blood. Not a second later the bottom of his cloak was pulled up, put on his face to cover it.

"I think it's time you leave now." Her voice was barely higher than a whisper, much as it had been a couple minutes ago. Except this time there was no emotion, no sorrow, no anger. Her brother scoffed, shook his head. He walked slowly to his horse with his head up, trying to stop the blood flow. She just stood there and watched him walk away, knowing there was nothing she could do.

"Theo?"

He paused.

"You can tell my nieces that I'm going into the service of Canberran Pirate Lord Selker. I won't be back for a long time. Our father's dog will be going to Uncle Hendred's house. He offered to pay the fee of the pirate lord if I give him the dog."

Theo stayed still for a moment longer before continuing over to his horse, hopping onto it and clutching the cloak to his face.

If she had any more emotion left in her, she would have laughed as he awkwardly grasped the reins with one hand.

But Theo had ridden off, and he was never going to come back.

There was nothing Ana could do but seethe and contemplate at that bench, so she wandered off back to the port. Her bag was on the ship, filled with the only belongings she had left. A few shirts, pants, skirts, a hunting dagger, her father's sword from service, his war horn, and her mother's necklace. She had thrown her own sword into the ocean and burned her cloak that the Oakgroven navy had given her the night before.

The men stared at her, murmuring about a woman on the ship. She knew they would talk, and it had almost prevented Lord Selker from accepting her into his service. Greed had won out though. She fought against three of his men and bested them all. Her father had them both join the Oakgroven Navy for five years before…

Before her mother died. Before they were allowed to be honorably discharged. Before her father went on drinking binge every other day and, by some miracle, before they began to run out of money. It was before all that, she found her skills on the sea were more than just suited to a fishing boat. She had eventually convinced him to become a merchant but… But that failed.

Part of her father had died when her mother did. He couldn't truly live on without her. But despite that, she was highly trained at sea. She had sworn her oath to the sea goddess when she was a young girl and had always called it home.

She walked down into the hull of the ship, running her hand over the salt worn wood.

On this ship, she wasn't Analise, the mentally unstable poor girl of Oakgrove.

She could be… Whoever she wanted to be, she supposed. But who was that?

A man stopped her. "Woman, this ship is not meant for folk like you. It's best if you get going." Analise turned towards the man, leveling him with a stare she had once given to pirates like him when she was fighting against them.

Now she was a pirate herself, no better than the ones she had hunted.

The Canberran Pirates were infamous. Certain ports paid them to protect their assets and keep the riffraff out. They could be loved in one port and feared in the next. Analise knew that if she wanted a fresh start, she was going to place herself in service of the most legendary armada that ever sailed.

"I'm right where I need to be. Where is Lord Selker?" Analise focused on that professionalism that had advanced her career far in the navy. She gripped the hilt of the sword at her side and kept walking forward, shouldering him out of the way.

She wanted her first impression to be one to keep these men away from her. Analise only turned back to see his reaction and look to see if he gave her directions. The man blinked a few times, as if shocked by the behavior. He raised his hand, pointing a finger to the Captain's Quarters behind them. The man turned away, grumbling something about insufferable women while going to do some insignificant task.

And as she turned to head to the Captain's Quarters, the door opened behind her, and a voice drawled.

Lord Selker leaned against the doorframe, wearing a long robe over his clothes that she saw scholars wearing at the libraries in Oakgrove. "Ah, Analise, early, are you?" She nodded, keeping that same look on her face. The picture next to the definition of calm, she told herself. Despite her jittery nerves. Analise may have been skilled at sea, but Lord Selker was a Pirate Lord. She wouldn't be surprised if he had been born on the sea. He was as infamous as they came, waging battles all over the oceans of Tarlatan. He beckoned her in, closing the doors behind them to drone out the sounds on the deck.

"Forgive my informal wear, I prefer to be comfortable while looking over maps and deciding our next location." Lord Selker sat in the chair behind his desk, resting his arms on the arms of the chair and keeping one foot propped out. She would have snorted- an infamous Pirate Lord who pillaged cities on a good day and razed them to the ground on a bad day, preferring a robe to be comfortable. But she kept that thought to herself, merely taking a seat across the desk from him.

"I am indeed early, Lord Selker. I apologize- I unfortunately have no money for a room at the inn and my cottage is a day's journey from here. I wished to come early and get my orders ahead of time so I may get started early." She stayed ramrod straight in her chair, not daring to lean back. Lord Selker just watched her for a moment, as if studying her.

He leaned back completely in his chair, putting his feet up on his desk. "There are many things I would like you to do, Analise, but for now, I shall settle with you being a chef." Analise started, ready to rip into him- she had been on the ocean for five years in the Oakgroven Navy, spent three as a merchant, and had sailed on the sea with her family when she was a child. To be placed as a chef... But Lord Selker cut her off before she could get a word out. "I understand you are likely expecting more. The moment I heard you start asking about me at the ports, I had my men investigate you. You are skilled, but I need to make sure my investment in you is sound."

Investment in her? She had paid him, for god's sake. But Analise pursed her lips, plastering on a fake smile and nodded.

Over the next few years, Analise rose in importance to Lord Selker. She served on his ship from the start so he could personally oversee her training.

A trick to keep the men in line, he said.

She, at first, was just cleaning the deck, cooking food, doing inventory, and washing the clothing. The men eventually became to her and paid no attention to her. Analise still didn't know who she wanted to be, so she didn't cause trouble. She kept to her duties, took on more as they were given to her, and didn't dare speak up at meals or roll call in the morning.

It seemed like it was just simple chores, but she eventually became Lord Selker's spy. Certain men, he said, he could not trust. They were better than an empty spot on the ship, despite being scraped from the bottom of the barrel. In the kitchens and washrooms, there was more gossip than a brothel. If the men underestimated her, they would not think to avoid speaking around her.

As time went on, Lord Selker began to have her train with his night shift. They were his most trusted and experienced pirates, utterly loyal to him and no one else. When they rolled into ports to pillage cities that did not pay the Canberran Pirates, Lord Selker let her loose. They would sit off the coast and row into shore when it was night, and the people on shore were too sleepy or drunk to notice them. It was just her and the men that trained her. He let her fight alongside the men, steal gold and jewels and finery, and raid taverns for additional stores. When they raided ships during the day, he kept her in the kitchens. Lord Selker did not want his men knowing how skilled she was just yet, he said.

But then, one morning, an Oakgrove ship was spotted patrolling and began sailing towards them. Lord Selker always had a particular hatred of the Oakgroven Navy... One of the reasons Analise had chosen to go into service under him.

"Lord, do you want us to steer away and lower the sails for more speed?" His First Mate called out, almost sounding bored. Knowing what the outcome would be but asking so no one could say he had led them into the mess that was about to ensue.

Lord Selker bore a feral smile. "No, let them come. I want to see if Oakgroven blood paints the water as red as it has in the past, or if it now reflects the blackness in their souls." Analise mirrored his smile and clutched the rail of the ship, eagerly watching.

She would get her retribution against Oakgrove for the trouble they had caused her family. It had been years since they had encountered an Oakgroven ship- and she would not let the opportunity for revenge pass.

"Don't look so happy. Selker will likely let a girl like you go if it means he can get a fight started." The man next to her nudged her side. He was one of the ones who treated her as though she was incapable of doing the duties of a man while trying to say that he respected her.

"I am not for sale or loan. If Selker wants a chef that won't poison his men, he'll keep me safe." Analise, not for the first time since she had declared service to Lord Selker, bore a stare of hardened steel and turned to face the man. She flipped him off before walking away, heading towards the top deck to resume cleaning.

As she walked up the stairs, an arm flew out in front of her. Selker. "Ah, there's that fire that convinced me to let you join our ship. Excited for Oakgroven blood, eh?" He caressed her arm, letting his fingers travel up the side of her face before she pushed his arm away.

She gave him that same look of hardened steel before walking away. Lord Selker always said it was an act, to keep the men from harming her. If they thought she was his prize, they wouldn't touch her. They would also think she was harmless, if their Lord did nothing but put her in the kitchens and flirt with her.

But sometimes she couldn't tell the difference between the ruse and reality, so every time she ignored those advances. She went into the service of one of the most legendary Pirate Lords to ever live for one reason, and one reason only. That reason was not to flirt.

"I wouldn't walk away so fast. I need you to do something." She paused, dread entering her heart. Perhaps that man hadn't been wrong.

"What is it, Lord?" Ana hadn't wanted to say the words but didn't want to catch more attention than she had already gotten.

Lord Selker strode forward, twirling a lock of hair around his finger. She yanked her head away, staring him in his eyes. He grabbed her hair firmer, pulling her forward. "Don't forget whose service you're in. Just because you've been quiet, doesn't mean you aren't here. You take orders from me. Now, you're going to go downstairs and change into a skirt, frilly blouse, and one of those pairs of stays that women wear. You're going to put on a billowing cape, put your hair into a ragged bun, and pretend to be a woman stolen by pirates. Beneath that cape will be a sword, which you'll use to cut down the Captain of that Oakgroven ship." He still gripped her hair, staring into her eyes- waiting for her to bow down.

But Ana had sworn a long time ago to bow to no one. She stared him in the eyes and nodded. "Aye, Captain." He gripped her hair tighter for a moment before letting her go, pushing her in the direction of the stairs.

Despite the dread that had crept into her heart, the excitement of her retribution fueled a fire she hadn't felt in a long time. She gladly donned the skirt, blouse, and stays. Beneath the blouse, she wrapped the leather belt around so that it would hang enough behind her hips to be unseen. The sword was sheathed, and she pulled her dark brown hair into a somewhat respectable, albeit ragged, bun that represented a married woman. When she looked into a mirror she had taken from a brothel, she practiced a doe eyed look that would make the Captain take one look at her brown eyes and think nothing else of her.

"For you, father…" She whispered to herself, before steeling her nerves and heading back upstairs.

Over the next few hours, she adopted the quiet, meek personality of a woman who had been taken from her husband. Anytime anyone looked at her, she wouldn't stare them in the eyes. She only stared longingly across the sea, towards nothingness… Towards her freedom, had she been that woman taken against her will.

Some of the men, unsurprisingly, took up the act and went along with it as well. Calling her slurs, degrading her, one even daring to hit her.

He was thrown into the brig, gagged to not shout and warn the Oakgroven ship when it got here. The rest of the men degrading her quieted after that.

Deep in her soul, her blood was boiling and desperate to get revenge against Oakgrove. For denying the payment that had been owed to their family and not letting them leave until *after* her mother had died. Perhaps... Perhaps if she and Father had been able to leave sooner, before mother died, her brother might not have hated her father so much.

The Oakgroven ship came closer and closer with each passing hour before it was finally close enough for those soldiers to board. Those hours had been torturous for Analise, having to pretend to be a meek woman. She had fought so hard to be the opposite of the type of woman she was pretending to be- helpless. Those hours had been equally torturous for the pirates around her. While the Canberran pirates were the picture of ease, she saw the frustration under their skin.

If the Oakgrove Captain noticed it, he would assume they were just frustrated as though they had been boarded by the navy a thousand times before. As if it was something taking up their time, when they could have gone elsewhere and pillaged for money.

Of course, it wasn't truly fruitless- they always slaughtered the sailors and enveloped their ships into the Canberran Armada. But this Oakgroven Captain didn't need to know that.

It was ironic, Analise thought to herself bitterly, that they sailed on an Oakgroven ship that now served under Canberran colors.

The Captain of the Oakgroven ship- Mistress' Fortune, they called it- walked the plank onto the Canberran ship. A mermaid was carved into the prow of the ship, a piss poor attempt to keep sirens away. She stared down the mermaid and developed a shake that she poorly tried to hide. Analise hid her face further into her hood and whispered prayers to any god she could think of.

"Lord Selker, what a pleasure it is to meet with you again. Last time we saw each other, you were facing charges in Oakgrove, no? Illegally trading?" The Captain ran his hand along the railing of the ship, as if he knew who it once sailed under. He raised his lip in disgust at the colors it was painted and pulled his hand away.

Lord Selker grinned, but it was a dark sort of grin. Neither happiness nor anger lit his eyes. He just stared down the Captain with a grin that would have had most falling to their knees and begging for forgiveness. "And I believe your King saw the gold it brought to his country and decided that, just this once, he would let a Canberran Pirate Lord off his shores. It had been a while since Oakgrove had seen that much gold, I suppose."

The Captain sneered, looking over the men on the ship. He inspected every surface.

"May I ask what you're looking for, Captain?" Lord Selker stayed at his place, standing on the top deck, and staring down. Staring down into the serpent's den.

The captain stopped before her, kneeling. "We received reports from an anonymous source that a woman had been taken captive by the Canberran pirates, away from her husband. When we tracked him down, he was worried sick. We've been stopping every Canberran ship we come across." She stilled. They had received reports. Had this been planned? She didn't let the surprise come to her face and she didn't dare look up to Selker in question. Oh, he would get an earful from her later. "My lady, are you here on this ship of your own free will?"

Analise shook even harder. She tried to still herself, but that only made her hands tremble even harder. Or that was what the captain saw. She opened her mouth a little and closed it again. Peeked out from under her hood and looked at him, but not in the eyes.

"I- I am, my lord." She shook her head against the words only a little, as if she was hoping the pirates wouldn't see. There were two men to either side of her, one behind her, and the captain in front of her.

The captain wiped the sneer from his face, placing a light smile on his face.

Analise wanted to cut it off his face. No- rip it off his face.

"My lady, I sense that life on the sea is not one for you. Would you like to join me on my ship instead? It may be nicer than that of a pirate ship." Analise dared to try to look up at Selker but whipped her head back. "I promise that they have no hold over you here. If you wish to leave, you may, my lady."

Analise trembled, but stood slowly, taking the hand that the captain stretched out towards her. They took a few steps before she found the knot in the wood that she avoided every day and fell to the ground.

She whispered out that she was sorry, struggled to get up and brushed her hands against the sides of her skirt. The Captain told her that there was no need to apologize and held out a hand to her, which she took again.

But her other hand was still on the grip of her blade, and she used the hand the Captain offered her to propel herself up...

And plunged her fathers sword into his heart.

She would have savored the absolute shock on his face if it was not for the soldiers surrounding her. She was upon them in a moment, barely hearing the other soldiers storming onto the ship.

Analise slashed and stabbed, blood pooling on the decks. She grimly thought she'd have to clean that later, too. She and the pirates worked together like a well-oiled machine, taking down Oakgroven sailors. They'd done this time and time again on shore, but never had Selker made her take the lead. Something was different this time and her blood sung at it.

A presence behind her- she whirled, almost upon them in an instant, but her blade paused at Selker's face before hers.

She breathed heavily, panting from the action.

But she continued the movement with her blade, his blows matching her own. Analise pushed him back till he was up against the door to his cabin, a grin on his face. She pulled the dagger out of the sheath at his side and stabbed it into the wood next to him.

"You will *never, ever* do that again without telling me. You will let me know if there are rumors where I am the center of attention. And you will always *ask me first.*" She hissed out the words, unsheathing a dagger and pressing it against his throat. The prick still had that smirk on his face- the fighting behind her had stopped, she noted.

Selker- the asshole- laughed. Then she remembered she had no status, and she was holding a blade to a pirate lord's throat. "What if I said that you'd take orders from no one but yourself?" Analise stilled every bone in her body. "Mistress' Fortune is yours. The six Pirate Lords converged five months ago. There are seven seas and six Pirate Lords. We need a seventh. You've worked on my ship for the past four years. You came to me, and I saw how broken you were- but strong. You did not beg to be in my service. You did not blush with embarrassment when you said your uncle would pay the fee to come into my service. It was not greed that won out when you offered your cut to my ship." Selker glanced down to the blade at his neck and back up at her.

Analise thought she left her body.

Her blade dropped to the ground. She took a couple steps back, the shaking in her hands real this time. "*What* is going on?"

Selker smiled. "You are the seventh Pirate Lord of Canberra, Analise. All of the men who have spent time training with you have told me it should be you since the day you stepped foot on this ship. You are a Commander of the Seven Seas." His smile- it was genuine. There was no mischief.

She thought over everything she had done in the last few years. Every port city she had helped sack. Every Oakgroven sailor she had helped take down. Every pot she scrubbed, deck she washed, and fish she had caught. Every single man she scared away with a single look that told them to *back off.*

"Mistress' Fortune... She is truly mine?" Analise gulped. Four years ago, she had nothing.

Now she was a Pirate Lord.

Selker nodded. She spun around, hearing scruffs behind her. Gods, they were *kneeling.* Even the men who had just degraded her were kneeling.

They would continue to kneel, every time she walked onto the deck of Mistress' Fortune. As a punishment to the men who had degraded Analise, he put them in her service for seven years. After those seven years were up, they would be dropped in a port and would never go into service under a Canberran Pirate Lord again. Analise would thoroughly enjoy every day of those seven years.

When they did get back to the Canberran Caves, Mistress' Fortunes was repainted. Analise smiled and gripped the rails of the ship she was on, smelling the salty sea air and the smoke coming out of the cave from cooking fires. It was their home when they were not at sea and held the closest thing Analise ever had to a family since...

Since her mother had died.

She kept the mermaid- but demanded they add claws and point out the fins. It would be no mermaid, but a siren. Analise was staring at the handiwork from another ship she was commanding when an albatross flapped noisily down onto the deck, a letter in a bottle strapped to its leg. One of her men tossed it a fish as she unstrapped the jar. It would remain on the deck until they either strapped a new letter on or commanded it to leave. It was the only way the Pirate Lords kept in communication with one another.

Analise pulled out the letter, leaning against the railing. She snorted, recognizing Selker's handwriting and the introduction. Ever the charmer... But her blood went cold at the words as she continued reading.

> Lord Analise-
>
> Four Pirate Lords are converging their armadas in the northern seas near the Ionian Mountains. One Pirate Lord will remain in the south, one will remain in the west, and one will remain in the east. I will be one of four as well as you.
>
> You have been chosen to be the representative of the Pirate Lords at the meeting in the Ionian Mountains. You are to organize your ships and join your fleet with the other three Pirate Lords. I know you keep your armada close- call upon them now, every single ship. Do not leave a single one behind.
>
> There... We have been told there is a great evil coming upon this continent. It started with Luce Stellarum and Statium. For a moment, the world held a bated breath that maybe the evil was satiated.
>
> A great host is being assembled to combat this

evil. It seems even the Canberran Pirates will be needed in this fight.

Analise, everyone is threatened by this evil. We must protect them all, even Oakgrove. You must come with all haste.

She crumbled the note and threw it in the ocean, eyeing the albatross who cocked its head as it looked at her.

"Don't give me that look." The albatross squawked a little before pitter pattering off to another area of the ship, likely looking for more fish.

Her First Mate, Cartha, stalked up to her and frowned. "What's wrong, Lord?"

"Four Pirate Lords are converging their armadas around the Ionian Mountains in the North Sea. I have been chosen to represent the Pirate Lords at a meeting being held." Cartha went deathly still. "Selker says there is a great evil coming to this continent. That it didn't just end after the Great Fire of Statium. It was just merely... A breath being held." Analise loosed a sigh, pinching the bridge of her nose.

She looked down to the deck below her, staring across the sea. Analise wondered what evil was coming- and how, exactly, it would affect her men. Cartha did the same, eyes wide, hand gripped on her sword handle.

"And now the breath is being released..." Cartha murmured, her voice barely above a whisper. Analise nodded grimly- didn't have the words for anything else. "When do we leave?"

You must come with all haste.

Analise felt the wind shift, the sails- despite being up- bristling, begging to be released. They were moored just outside the Canberran caves, resupplying and visiting family before going off to sea again. Her entire fleet was here and could leave in a moment's notice.

The horn at her hip felt heavy. She had adopted the custom from the Oakgroven navy amongst her own fleet and had added a metal lip to the top of the horn, carved with symbols of the sea goddess Scylla. To ring this horn... It was only meant to rally her men and act as a call to arms in desperate times.

She had promised her father she would only use the horn if it was truly needed, when she added the metal lip to his horn.

She released it from her hip, gripped it in her hands. The men on board stilled, gradually turning towards her.

And then she blew the horn as loud as she could. Not once-but three times. A call to arms at all haste.

The Canberran Pirates would answer the call.

CHAPTER 3

THE FALLEN SENTINEL

HER HEART WAS POUNDING LOUDLY- IN THE DARK OF NIGHT, IT was the only sound to be heard for what seemed like miles. Or maybe that was just her paranoia kicking in as she slinked into the dark alleyway, her hand moving slowly towards her dagger. Just a moment ago she had heard a shrill scream that ended rather quickly and muffled, and being the good samaritan she was, had decided to investigate. As every second passed, she was regretting this decision but kept her stance defensive and mouth shut.

But even her own instincts couldn't prevent the startled gasp that came out at the mutilated corpse in front of her. She hadn't even taken thirty seconds to get back here and whoever caused the shrill scream couldn't be seen. Which meant the killer was either still close by or had magic.

There was a snap behind the crate next to her.

Her hand shot to her dagger and held it in front of her, backing up towards a wall and down towards the entry to the alley. She wasn't even supposed to be here in the first place.

She clenched one hand into a fist to keep it near her face. A figure slowly stood from behind the crate, growing until it towered over her. The figure made a low, deep growl starting at a mere whisper, but eventually turned into a noise that made her wince in pain as it bounced off the walls. Everything about this whole situation made her heart rise into her throat with a fear she would refuse to show. She squared her own shoulders as best she could in a defensive stance, turned her face into a steel mask, and held her dagger in a firm grip.

Gods, she wished she had more than this dagger. She had left her sword at home by the order of her commander. Even the leather armor... She worried it was not enough.

Just a social visit. You're scary enough.

She would have snorted if this figure hadn't just killed someone. She wasn't sure if she was *scary enough* to the figure in front of her. It took a few steps closer to her, but not close enough that she could make him out.

Whatever it was, she should have seen it by now. It was as if the alley was cloaked in complete darkness. This would not be how she died- in a dark alleyway cornered by a man twice her size. Red eyes peered at her in the darkness. One more step was taken by the figure before he disappeared into thin air. She swung with her dagger in front of her, but only caused a faint whistling noise. Cautiously, she took on a normal position, but still held the dagger firm.

A pigeon cooed on one of the roofs above.

She needed to get back to the inn- no, she needed to get back to her commander and let them know that there was a body here. But... She was also curious as to what had killed the person. The body was left so mutilated she couldn't tell whether it was a woman or a man- the hair that was pulled out was long, blonde, and curly locks. It was the only indication to her that it may have been a woman. A ring was left on her right hand- wouldn't the killer have wanted to take that? And more importantly, a bag was left on the ground. Still clasped together, untouched, and in perfect condition.

Parts of the body were singed. Odd amounts of dust and ash surrounded the body, but she dismissed it. Probably just ashes from the body with the amount of burnt bits. Her auburn hair fell in her face as she rubbed her eyes. It had been a long day...

Daenestra walked back down the alley and onto the street. She looked both ways- no sign of any soldiers. She looked back at the body and pinched the bridge of her nose.

Fuck.

Ten minutes later, Daenestra walked out of the alley with the body over her shoulder wrapped in a burlap sack and the bag, hair, dust, and ashes stuffed into her own bag. She made a mental note to send the receipt for a bag to replace her own to the command. And when she did walk into the barracks, she promptly put the body onto the table in the entry.

"Daenestra... What the hell is that?" The Desk Sergeant furrowed her brows and sniffed a little before holding her nose. "What the *hell* did you put on my desk?!"

Daenestra held up her finger and dropped the bag onto the desk next to the body. "Winter solstice present. I'll be giving you the receipt for a new bag." She walked towards her commander's office, ignoring the sputtering Desk Sergeant.

"You do know it's not even winter, right?" Her commander asked as she closed the door.

"Yeah, but the Sergeant's had a stick up her ass for months. She had it coming if you ask me." Daenestra shrugged and sat on the table. "Commander... I've never seen anything like it. Fae blood runs through me, and the most I could make out was its eyes. The body... Completely mutilated. Its scent is completely scattered. Not to mention all the dust and ash. It was almost impossible to detect anything."

In Daenestra's two hundred and twenty-three years of life, she had never faced a foe like that. Not even when Luce Stellarum fell. But the scent of the figure... No, she would not think back to that time.

Her commander frowned and looked out the window in her door before looking back at Daenestra. "Did any of it feel familiar?"

"That evil is long gone." She snorted and pushed off the desk. "My sisters and I made sure of it. I'll be back in the morning. Keep your staff armed."

Before she could walk out the door, her commander called to her. "Daenestra, we both know that kind of darkness lurks until it can be burned out. Luce Stellarum wasn't the first and it won't be the last. Promise you'll try to think if anything seems familiar."

No- she wouldn't try. That had remained locked away for a long time. "I'll do my best."

The walk to the inn was a long one. Daenestra had vowed to herself for so very long that she would never forget the sacrifices of her sisters, but that she would never return to that moment. But even she had to admit, that sort of darkness had not been seen since Luce Stellarum fell and Statium's capital, Hallenfall, burned to the ground.

Her home, Luce Stellarum, had been the gem of the world. Her gleaming cities of gold and marble had streets engineered for efficiency and speed. The capital, Averell, was a bustling port that welcomed anyone and everyone. The entire country housed libraries, museums, theaters, and universities. It contained anyone from artists and scholars to warriors and politicians to healers and families. It had buildings that touched the sky and temples to all the twenty-five gods.

Even the poorest family in Luce Stellarum was not ignored- the Queen gave small amounts out of the treasury each month to those families rather than making them pay taxes. Countries all over the main continent called those citizens lazy and just "looking for a handout". But the Queen... Her people were her pride and joy. In her eyes, she was investing in them. If they were able to bring themselves out of poverty and begin making money, it would only bring more wealth to Luce Stellarum. And two hundred and twenty-four years ago, the Queen of Luce Stellarum decided that she would provide her people with the best warriors the world had ever seen.

The Queen journeyed to the Fae Kingdoms of the East, bartering with their rulers. If they would allow some of the Luce Stellarum men to have children with the Fae women, Luce Stellarum would provide lucrative trade deals and send over their artisans to live amongst the Fae. Within a year, a thousand babies were born and, by some strange stroke of magic, were all female. They remained in the Fae Kingdoms for fifty years, where they trained as warriors and learned the history of the world. The Queen lived amongst them until it was her time to return to Luce Stellarum. In time, another Queen came along to retrieve her army. She received a deadly army that had sworn an oath to protect Luce Stellarum until their death.

For another one hundred and twenty-three years, Luce Stellarum lived in peace. The Queen had named these deadly women Sentinels in reminder to the rest of the world that these women were watching. But all that is good must eventually come to an end.

The military scouts began seeing strange ships floating in the ocean- unmanned, seemingly abandoned. Every time the scouts got close enough, the ships would disappear. The Queen was unnerved and rightfully so. With Statium having closed its borders in fears of an evil approaching, she began to wonder if she should do the same. But Luce Stellarum was not full of cowards, and she would not close their borders if the rest of the world needed help.

Daenestra staggered to a stop. She remembered every bit of this like it was yesterday. In a sense, it was. Fifty years had gone by in the blink of an eye. Having the lifespan of a Fae would do that, she supposed. A man atop a horse yelled at her—she took a step back, reminding herself to stay focused. She waved to the man, apologizing, before going around the horse so he might continue.

She missed Luce Stellarum. She missed the clean streets and friendly faces. The kingdom of Corsair left much to be desired, and the people were less than friendly. But they were the only ones on the main continent who had offered refuge to the Sentinels free of charge. Some of her sisters did join her, but most journeyed back to the Fae Kingdoms despite their betrayal.

The inn... The inn was as good as they came in Corsair. It was the nicest one she could find and offered monthly pricing rather than night to night. The barmaids were about as honest as the snake oil salesmen and the food tasted like it came from the gutter, but it was a place to sleep. The King of Corsair had offered to give them homes and land in exchange for service under his banner, but Daenestra couldn't stomach it. She served one kingdom no matter if it had fallen or not. Instead, she became a mercenary, hiring herself out to low level commanders in the larger cities who needed her help.

Daenestra didn't bother stopping at the bar. She continued up to her room, slipping off her boots and staring down the silver armor in the corner. She kept it polished and pristine, ready for the day when her Queen would call her back.

Not that she knew if the queen was even *alive* to call her back. Those ships that had disappeared had come back to form a fleet that would crush Luce Stellarum. It contained an army that would overrun the main continent, not only Luce Stellarum. All the commanders had gathered at the table, trying to decide what to do.

"Statium refuses to help. They sent us a letter back saying that 'They told us this day would come and we should have done the same'. Rosenfall

is too far to call for aid. Corsair is focusing on readying their defenses should they be next in line." The commander of the army looked at the list in front of him. "Oakgrove had soldiers on their way for training already, but they are estimated to still be a week away. Any other kingdom has not yet responded. On top of that, the enemy has fired upon the bridge to the mainland and collapsed it to prevent any sort of evacuation. We are alone." The room was somber, lit by candlelight and moonlight streaming in from the windows.

The Queen remained silent while her naval commander spoke. "Our fleet is surrounded on the western side. We will never be able to escape and we can't outmaneuver them either. The Fae Kingdoms already refused aid as well, saying that our Sentinels should be enough. They did add that if any Sentinels wished to return to the Fae Kingdoms, they would allow them in."

Daenestra was in disbelief. They had been living in peace her entire life. She had expected small skirmishes here and there, maybe a territorial dispute, or even a war with a lesser kingdom. But these ships… She had never seen anything like them. When she ventured out on a ship and got close enough, she could smell the darkness and evil rolling off those ships. It would be a miracle if they survived that evil. And now, her family was denying her aid.

"What if there was another ally?" The Queen murmured. Her three commanders perked up in confusion. "A Canberran Pirate Lord has a fleet in the east not too far away. If we can send a messenger, they might be able to get here in time."

"Your Majesty, the Canberran Pirate Lords have never gone as far as allying themselves with a kingdom. They are on no one's side but their own. How do we know if we can trust them?" The naval commander spoke slowly, as if he was realizing it was their only option.

The Queen smiled. Her brown hair was set in a braid and a crown lay atop her head. "Privateer, I don't believe trust is a luxury we have anymore."

"You'll still need someone to hold back the enemy. We can get everyone to the eastern side of the island, but if they think we've moved, they'll just

move to attack us in a different area." The military commander frowned. "I think even if the Canberran Pirates help, it's still a losing battle."

Daenestra knew she wasn't leaving this island and smiled with the Queen. "If the Sentinels remain in Averell, the enemy will never know you aren't here. My Queen, you'll take the entirety of our military and our citizens. I shall leave five Sentinels with you in case something should happen. You won't be using the Canberran Pirate fleet to fight for you, they'll be ferrying you somewhere this evil can't find you." Daenestra spoke, not an ounce of fear in her voice. If this was to be the end, so be it.

"If we do this, we'll remain in the Canberran Pirate's debt." The military commander snapped.

"If we don't do this, we won't be around to worry about debts, General." The Queen turned to Daenestra and held her hand on her face. "My friend, we've been through so much together. This isn't what my great grandmother envisioned for your life. We will not judge you or your Sentinels if you do not want to stay behind."

They both knew that was a future that could never be. "This isn't what she envisioned for our life, but it is what she envisioned for our death. My Queen, it has been a pleasure serving your family. We swore an oath to protect Luce Stellarum until our last breaths. The Sentinels will hold that oath." Daenestra smiled, placing her hand on top of the Queens.

A tear fell down the Queen's face. "We will leave behind three of the fastest ships from the Canberran pirates for you and whatever Sentinels remain. Promise me that you'll live."

"I've already made an oath to fight to the death. It's a little difficult to make an oath to live, as well."

There hadn't been much discussion after that. The country fell into chaos. The Sentinels organized the evacuation of Averell, while the rest of the military organized the evacuation of the rest of Luce Stellarum. Overnight, the entire country had made it to the other side of the island. Some likely remained out of stubbornness, and some were slow with old age and weakness. The remaining citizenry that made it to the ships would board and wait a week for the Sentinels. If none came... They were ordered to find the rest of the fleet.

Daenestra settled onto the bed and flipped over, looking away from the armor. She instead studied the candle and its dying flame. It dully lit the room, casting a faint glow that made Daenestra cry. She had spent many nights with her Queen, laughing in the Library of Averell with that same, faint flow the only light. She had spent many nights with her sisters sitting around campfires, telling ghost stories and the legends of the Fae.

Now she sat alone in her room, her sisters scattered around the world, and her Queen... Somewhere. Daenestra couldn't- wouldn't- bring herself to say think of the possibility that she was dead. After nearly fifty years, Daenestra knew it was unlikely her Queen was still alive.

The fight that followed the evacuations had been brutal. The moment dawn broke out, the enemy fleet moved in towards the city. The Sentinels waited with bated breath for every minute that passed, staring down those row boats. Some ships were brave enough to dock right in their ports and didn't even bother with long boats.

For two long days and two long nights, the thousand Sentinels fought with every ounce of life in their bodies. Eventually, they were pushed out of the city and into the country- side. Part of Daenestra had been relieved when that happened- if anyone wanted to run, wanted to escape, they had the opportunity here. They could run into the tunnels used by farmers for storage and wait out the army above.

Eventually... The Sentinels numbered only three hundred. They were bloodied and their silver armor dinged, dented, and scratched. Some pieces were missing entirely. Their leather faulds were torn and ripped. But, they had managed to work the enemy towards a pass, where it funneled the numbers and made it possible to hold them off for longer. Shields were their greatest ally at that point- spears had long been spent by then.

Daenestra shuddered. She remembered it all so clearly. The creatures... They were beasts more fearsome than any she had ever been taught about by the Fae. They were utterly demonic, with no indiscernible soul. Whoever created them... Daenestra had no idea who had the power to control the beasts.

By that point, the enemy was gaining on them. They entered their ranks and tried to tear through them. The Sentinels were growing tired and had little left in them. Daenestra saw the sun setting behind them and knew most would not last the night, if any.

She slashed and stabbed around her, taking down enemies left and right. She looked around, spinning in the chaos. All her training could not have prepared her for the chaos of this moment. Her Sentinels needed to rally, needed a second bout of strength if they were to last any longer. She grabbed the flag of Luce Stellarum and stabbed it into the ground, looking around at her Sentinels.

The light was fading behind them and the Fallen Kingdom. They strengthened the grips on their swords and fought to reform their shaky lines.

They stared down the enemy once more...

And roared a battle cry that shook the very core of the world.

The enemy paused, as if feeling that ground quake beneath them. They ran, ran, ran down their enemy and fought as the world had never seen anyone fight before. If the original Queen who had bartered for their lives had seen them now, she might have cried. Most of the Sentinels were crying with rage and battle fury.

Daenestra knew that rallying cry would wane though, and fought harder with each passing minute. The enemy hadn't made it behind them. The enemy wouldn't get behind them. But gods... They never stopped coming. She hadn't slept in three days and only drank in quick swigs. She had stuffed a piece of bread in her mouth when the enemy had given them an odd but brief respite and just… Stood there.

Now, she didn't feel hunger. No, a killing fury had taken over her body. She was a whirling tiger with her twin blades, shield thrown to the side by now, and they were her prey.

A Sentinel ran up to her. "Commander, we can't last much longer. I can't be sure, but I estimate there are one hundred and fifty of us left. Leave behind fifty of us and let us block them so that the rest may live."

That promise rang through her head- 'Promise me that you'll live'.

"I can't ask you to do that."

The Sentinel smiled. "It's a good thing you aren't asking and I am. It's been an honor to fight under you. Until we meet again in the never-ending sky, Daenestra."

Daenestra hadn't the heart to answer. She only fought harder, calling for a retreat as the fifty Sentinels formed a line of shields across the pass and planted their feet into the ground. Those Sentinels gave them the ten precious minutes they needed to sprint across the countryside, find an obscure tunnel hidden amongst brush, and run as far as they could in the tunnels.

Eventually, on the sixth day, they had made it to the ships. To her relief, they were still there, with the remainder of the citizenry waiting on them. One ship was full of the citizens, and a small number of Sentinels went to join the fleet. Daenestra and the rest dispersed amongst the two other ships, headed for the main continent. They would come back when it was safe and honor their sisters. They vowed it upon the blood they had spilled into the earth. But until then… They would keep other kingdoms safe.

Daenestra blew out the candle, closed her eyes, and found for the first time in years, a dreamless sleep.

The next morning, Daenestra woke up and stared down the silver, shining armor. She had gotten it repaired, but mainly wore leather armor now. That was set off to the side, hastily

removed in the middle of the night. She knew once she put on
that armor, she would set herself onto a path that she couldn't
turn back on.

But still, she put on that armor, piece by piece. Every piece
put on, despite the weight, felt like stones lifted off her heart.
She donned her leather faulds, strapped her twin blades to her
side. Her shield had never been taken from the pass- she had
thrown it down and never had a second thought about it. But
her cloak had survived, a gift from the original queen whose
dream to create an army to protect Luce Stellarum had
paid off.

She gripped the fabric, two hundred and twenty-three
years old, and let her tears fall onto it. The bottom was torn,
dirty, and stained with blood. She hadn't been able to look at it,
never mind get it repaired. This was Fae fabric, woven so
tightly that she could have sworn magic was woven with it. It
kept out all water, wind and cold. The Queen had ordered the
cloaks dyed with the cerulean blue color of the royal house and
embroidered with a sun, to symbolize the light that they would
always fight in. Next to the cloak was the clasp made of a
sword and twisting vines. The Queen had given it to only her, a
symbol of her command.

Putting on this cloak would send a signal to the entire
world.

But she put it on anyway, clasping it at her shoulder and
storming through the door.

The tavern was bad enough, but the moment she stepped
onto the street in her shining armor and blue cloak, the streets
murmured with curiosity. Stories milled through the streets,
recognizing the clasp and the embroidered sun. When she
walked into the office, she didn't entertain the Desk Sergeants
sputtering and breezed right past her into her Commander's
office.

"I take it you're the reason the streets are buzzing with

news of the Commander of the Sentinel's return?" The Commander asked warily, looking over the armor and wicked twin blades at both of Daenestra's sides.

"I'm not wearing the clasp and cloak for nothing." Daenestra didn't offer up more than that before leaning against the wall and throwing a bag of gold onto the desk. "I'll be leaving. Here is the gold you paid me for my service."

The commander pocketed the gold and noted something before looking up at her. "Have you had time to think about the body and the connection to Luce Stellarum?"

Daenestra nodded. "When I fought against whoever our enemy was, they had a scent to them- we got as close as we could before the battle, and it stunk like death. The scent last night was tainted because of the dead body, but that figure- it had the same smell. Not true death like that dead body but… Something different. Something I can't explain. But that evil wasn't gone- just regrouping." The commander gave her a soft look, something Daenestra ignored.

"Thank you, for thinking back. I'll have to alert the Council. They'll want to know as soon as possible. Where will you go?" The Commander asked.

Daenestra didn't want to reveal that yet. Unlike fifty years ago, trust was a luxury she *could afford*. "I must stop somewhere before finding my sisters. I want to see if they have seen similar things happening." The commander nodded and Daenestra strutted out before she could ask any more questions. The Desk Sergeant sputtered about something Daenestra didn't bother to pay attention to, and she snatched the letter that the Desk Sergeant was waving around at her. It was promptly stuffed into her pack, safe for the journey.

Daenestra walked to the port, commissioning a ship to take her to Luce Stellarum. Most avoided her, but one Captain balked at the Fallen Sentinel Commander and offered up his ship for free. His grandfather had met a Sentinel after the battle, he said, and would always remember how they defended Luce Stellarum and prevented Corsair from being fodder for the enemy next.

It was always the "enemy", Daenestra thought, looking out across the waves. She hadn't bothered to investigate it after the enemy had slinked away, but even Luce Stellarum with all of their knowledge hadn't been able to discover who exactly the enemy was.

But now... Maybe if she had caught this evil early enough, maybe she could figure out who the enemy was- and give another kingdom time to save their country. When she had woken up this morning and stared at her armor and cloak, she told herself that she knew she would always come back. It was why her armor was so pristine, she told herself. But in reality...

She felt guilty for leaving her sisters. Even when she was promoted to commander, she fought amongst her Sentinels. She lived with them as a common soldier, trained with them, fought with them.

She should have died with them too.

When the ship finally made it to Luce Stellarum, she ordered him to sail the boat along to the main port. Coming to this place... The island had all looked the same. As if they had never left and the enemy had never come. But if the enemy was still on the island, she'd be able to see their ships there. Eventually they determined the coast was clear, and they gave her a rowboat to go to the island. She ordered them to flee at the first sight of an enemy ship. She had sketched a crude model to give them an example.

Rowing towards the city was more difficult than she thought and not just because of the armor she wore. The city... She landed at the docks and tied her boat. The city was exactly how she remembered it before they were pushed out. Buildings destroyed; the precious marble cracked and scorched. The gold had melted in fires that had burned just as hot as the one in Hallenfall. Daenestra shivered- she wondered if they had planned to burn Averell to the ground and didn't expect the resistance. Perhaps putting down the resistance in Luce Stellarum was more effective than burning it to the ground.

Bones now littered the street, scavenged completely. Armor and swords from enemy and Sentinel alike remained, dull and lifeless. She kneeled and grabbed the dagger from a Sentinel. It was still as sharp as the day it was made- the beauty of Fae metal. She sheathed it in her boot, knowing how expensive it would be to purchase one of these in the Fae Kingdoms.

Just as the Canberran pirates had been ordered those fifty years ago, she had ordered her own Captain to remain there for a week. She was traveling to the pass to see what remained- if anything, of her fifty Sentinels.

She had to- she had to honor her sisters. Her blue cloak blew about in the breeze and out of the corner of her eye-

Daenestra fell to her knees. In that gods forsaken pass, the cerulean blue flag was still raised. Armor and bones were piled up around it, as if they had defended that flag until their last breath. She didn't bother to wonder why the enemy hadn't torn it down. Perhaps they didn't realize people would come back. Perhaps they didn't realize anybody would be crazy enough to return.

Daenestra sobbed harder there than she had the first night on the ship after the battle. After the battle, she screamed so loud she couldn't speak the next day. Her body was wracked with sobs, and her sisters joined her. The pirates had wisely stayed away as they mourned. Now she roared a battle cry, the same kind of battle cry she and the rest of those three hundred Sentinels had roared all those years ago.

She unsheathed that Fae dagger, slicing it across the meat of her palm. Dipping her finger in the blood, she stood and wrote in jagged script on a shield-

To those who wander by- remember the sacrifice of the fifty, and do not let their sacrifice be in vain.

A shield remained on top of all those bodies. She would not let their sacrifice be in vain and grabbed the shield from very top of the pile. Felt the fae magic pulse through it.

She somehow managed to pull herself together, drag herself back to the city, and return to the ship. When the Captain asked her where she wanted to go next, she ordered him to bring her back to Corsair. She would scour the country-side for her sisters.

"I found this letter blowing about your cabin- a porthole was left open. Thought you might want this." The Captain handed her the letter and returned to his post. The men on his ship left her alone as she unstrapped her armor and set it in her cabin. The letter had no name on the envelope but her own. She frowned and picked the wax seal off of the envelope and pulled the letter out as she walked back onto the main deck of the ship.

Daenestra covered her mouth with her hand.

Daenestra, Commander of the Sentinels, I, as the Queen of Luce Stellarum, order you to go to the Ionian Mountains. You are to organize the remaining Sentinels under your command.

My mother wanted to write this letter much earlier. She passed a few years ago but held a lot of love for you in her heart. The Canberran Pirate Lords called upon us for payment of that debt all those years ago. An army gathers- possibly the greatest the world will ever see. The world will need it if we are to defeat this evil.

It is a debt we will gladly pay. We will reclaim our home.

"Everything okay, Commander?" Daenestra looked down to the captain who was standing before her. He had a furrowed brow. Right- Daenestra was just standing there, mouth wide open.

"We need to turn around, Captain. We sail for the Ionian Mountains on order of the Queen of Luce Stellarum. But first, we're making a stop in a coastal city in Nazare. I have someone I need to find."

"The Queen?" The captain staggered back, but barked orders to his crew who flew into high gear. But then, as though a gear clicked into place, the captain spun around and faced her. "Commander, there are tales of a dragon in Nazare. Are you sure that's such a great idea?"

Daenestra gripped the sword at her side and smiled wickedly. "That's exactly the point, Captain."

CHAPTER 4

CREATURES OF THE NIGHT

"ALL I CAN REMEMBER IS HIM GOING AFTER ME WITH A DAGGER outside the village. I found a sword on the ground and killed him before he could stab me." She spoke aloud in the makeshift court. Almost… twenty years ago, the king had closed their borders and vowed to get rid of an evil seeping into their world. All manner of crime had been outlawed and now that she had killed someone, she was facing trial. The trial was really just for show to appease the people of Statium. No matter how the day ended, she would have the choice of being hung or having her head chopped off.

"Are you admitting to the murder?" The judge questioned. She snorted- even if she explained herself, they would execute her. So, she nodded, given no other option.

"I killed the man. It was in self-defense. Had I not killed him, you would have been staring him down today instead of me." She didn't bother pleading. She had been in this courtroom with her parents before to watch a trial. It was almost a form of entertainment for some. She had never seen the appeal in it, but had learned that pleading only led to death on site. If people thought that pleading could win them a way around the law, they'd exploit it as much as possible.

"Self-defense or not, a murder is a murder. You, Natalia Thatchen-croft, age 17, will be executed June 21st. Until then you will be staying in the dungeons of *Hallenfall awaiting execution. That is all.*" The judge slammed down the gavel, and guards grabbed Natalia's shoulders, shoved her up, and pushed her out of the room. She faintly heard her mother start choking back cries- heard her father whispering to her mother.

Then the pommel of a sword was smashed against the back of her head, and all went black.

Sometime later...

She awoke in the dungeons, shaking her head a little. It felt like it had been stuffed with cotton. Her heart was pounding in her ears and was startled by a guard rattling the door. She shuffled on the cot to the very edge, pressing herself against the wall.

"Your roommate for the next fifteen days." A guard with a gruff voice spoke aloud, pulling an older woman into view and shoving her into the cell. It looked as if she had a broken leg and a bruised rib. "Don't kill each other. The king will make an example of both your families if either of you die." The guard slammed the cell shut, locked it, and walked away. He burped loudly, patting his stomach.

"What a welcoming party." Natalia grumbled and moved away from the wall, shoving off the burlap sack they had given her as a blanket. Through the little bars, the sun began to rise and peek through.

"Well, by your tone of voice, it'll be a fun two weeks." The old woman announced, and Natalia smiled. The old woman would at least be a pleasant cellmate.

"Yeah, I'll be a ray of sunshine. Who wouldn't be excited for good food, comfortable blankets, and a guard who definitely doesn't look at you like a piece of meat..." Natalia held her head in her hands, gripping her head.

"Finally, someone who can joke around. What are you in for?" The old woman countered. Natalia looked back up and laughed.

"I killed someone. I had walked out of my village- I was going to meet a friend at a spot in the woods. We had planned it for months. I hadn't made it ten feet outside the gates before a man was holding a knife to my neck." Natalia breathed deeply before continuing. "We had just had a legion of Statium soldiers camping outside the village. One of them must *have left a sword behind. I fought my way out of his grip and lunged for the sword. I had never intended on using it but- I had swung my arm up and the sword plunged into his stomach. I didn't even have time to blink before he was dead."*

The old woman smiled understandingly. "I remember when the king made the punishment for all crimes to be execution. At first people couldn't believe it. Crime was rampant in Hallenfall, as if daring the king to hold to his word. And then..." That smile fell from the old woman's face. "Today they burn the bodies because there are no more fields left that can be used for graves. I told my grandchildren stories of what it used to be like." The old woman paused, coughing a little. Natalia grabbed a mug and filled it with water from the bucket in the cell. The old woman drank it slowly before continuing.

"When I killed... I was lucky enough to land in here with only a broken leg since I was just an old woman. The guards only saw their grandparents when they looked at me. Now they rotate me around under a different name each time. They created a medical record that I died, and I've been here ever since. I'm still not sure why they took pity on me, of all people." The old woman stopped, hearing the guard come walking back down the hall.

But then- shouting. Running. Natalia's blood ran cold and stood on the shaky cot, trying to see out the bars.

It wasn't the sun she had seen through those bars. It was a fire roaring over the capital. Her body chilled despite the blazing heat that began creeping into the cell. "What's going on out there?" The old woman asked, trying to peer up with her, but her legs could only lift her so far.

"Something very, very bad." Natalia had no other answer. She pressed her back against the door of the cell and turned around. "Help! We're locked in here!" She screamed so loud her lungs ached, shook the door so hard her arms felt like they'd fall off.

"They're not coming for us." The old woman whispered, settling onto her bed.

Natalia shook the bars, shook them until her hands melted with the bars and-

"Wake up, Natalia, wake up!" She was being shaken, shaken by big furry-

Big furry paws. With claws that stayed away from her skin.

Because her skin wasn't melting off from the inferno that burned the capital of Statium and the surrounding villages to the ground. She was in a bed in a cottage, being shaken awake by a shadow bear.

She gulped down air, sitting up on the bed. "I'm okay, Remy. I'm okay."

"Another dream?" The Shadow Bear plunked his butt on the ground, cocking his head. Concern filled his big golden eyes and Natalia rubbed her eyes clear of sleep.

"Yes. From before... Right before the fire. I didn't see my death but... I got right up to it. "

"It's never gone this far. You've gotten visions from your childhood, even killing that man but... The moment of your death? How is that even possible?" Remy tapped his claws against the ground, furrowing his brows.

Natalia threw herself back on the bed, groaning. "I wish I knew, Remy." She felt him climb onto the bed and lay next to her. When Natalia first started having nightmares as a child, she was too scared to sleep alone. Remy had a bigger bed made, one that could accommodate both if need be.

Not as a child, though. From what Natalia had gathered from her nightmares, she had been alive once before. Her and Remy spent weeks piecing it together, combing through books of magic and history, trying to find anything like it.

She had died and been reincarnated as a child. Whoever had reincarnated her, they had attempted to turn her into an ancient mockery of the fae known as a wraith. Beyond that... They had no idea. Her and Remy had no idea who had done it, where her body had been brought to after burning in Statium, and how she had ended up in the old man's cabin in the woods.

Natalia turned towards Remy and curled up against his side, gripping onto his black fur.

He had been there along with another that day, to save her. Remy wouldn't tell her who the old man was, and she barely remembered him beyond his wind magic, dark skin, white beard, and silver eyes. And yet, despite the white beard, the old man had run like the very wind carried him and spoke like he wasn't a day over thirty.

She had been lucky to be rescued that day. Ever since then, her and Remy had stuck together, bound by a soul tie. When Natalia had first met Remy, she had been fascinated. Her family had lived in a village on the outskirts of a forest. They had seen plenty of black bears before, but never a Shadow Bear.

Remy was massive and his fur dark as night. His eyes shimmered with gold like two stars in that expanse of night. When she found scars that littered his body and was worried he would die, he hushed her. He was an immortal, Remy explained. There was not much that could kill him and as long as she was alive, he would not leave her side.

When something did threaten her, he lashed out with claws as sharp as daggers. The day he found her, he had ripped her captor's head off and didn't even stop to think. He was a warrior as much as he was the only family she had left.

So much had happened that day- so much she had tried to forget. Natalia *wanted* to remember the old man. Wanted to cling onto every detail so that one day she might thank him. But then everything began to get fuzzy, and sleep fell upon her once again.

She blinked her eyes blearily, bringing her hand up to cover her eyes from the blinding light. She desperately tried to remember how she had gotten there but could only remember her name: Natalia Thatchencroft. Her small hands were tied together at her wrists and her ankles were bound as well. She was in the corner of a cabin. There were four windows and three doors- she noted them all. Which ones were closest, which ones obviously led to the outside.

How she knew to do this, she had no idea. But that thought was at the back of her head, with her focus on the man coming into view. He was short, had pale skin- had a large stomach. Not healthy.

But she was groggy, couldn't even speak to ask what was going on, and the man was coming at her so quickly. He grabbed her bound hands and some part of her remembered to fight even if her mind didn't. She bucked and pulled back, dug her heels into the ground all to no avail. The man pulled out a knife and held it to her throat. She felt her hair get trapped in his hands and before she could even be scared that she would do more than kill her…

The knife pulled away from her throat and was tugging at her hair just above her shoulders.

Long, black locks fell to the ground and turned to dust within seconds. She stared at them in horror. Like a piece of her that she didn't even know was important just… Disappeared.

The man, equally horrified, dropped the knife. "What the fuck?"

She took her opportunity and stomped her foot into his groin, running for the front door as quickly as she could, bursting through it without even thinking, not even noticing that she didn't have to open the door and –

Remy was roaring in her face, slobber landing all over it.

"Gods Remy! That's disgusting!" She pushed him away, wiping the slobber off.

"Natalia, you hadn't even been sleeping. What was this one about?" Remy frowned at her and plopped down again.

"Remy, I'm tired, I don't want to-"

"Natalia, it's getting worse. You have to talk to me."

She shot out of bed, shrugging on a cloak and whirling around to face him. "What do you want me to say, Remy? I know you feel the magic surge through me in all these nightmares. The magic that brings them back. I know you feel a part of me disappear every time I cut myself and the blood turns to ash before it hits the floor. And yet *we don't have any answers.*" Natalia stormed out the door, wanting to go anywhere other than here. She ran, whipping through the trees.

She heard Remy's thundering feet behind her. The ground shook with each of his steps, but she didn't care. She had one place in mind and was running to it. Natalia felt mist furling out behind her like great wings propelling her forward. It trailed behind her, wrapping around her, and her eyesight focused.

Then the lake came into view, and she had to slide to a stop to avoid running into it.

Natalia fell to her knees and *sobbed.*

She felt Remy slide to stop as well next to her.

He poked her shoulder with his nose, resting his head on hers. "It was him again, wasn't it?" All she could do was nod. "Natalia, it will be okay. One day, he will stop haunting you."

"And when he stops haunting me, another will replace him. These nightmares will never end." Her sobs wracked her entire body, mist curling up around her with each shake of her body. Remy pressed his head against her own and sighed.

"I'm eons old, child. My mother is in the never-ending sky with her siblings, and I will never see her again. I had a mate- her name was Ameniel. She… She died in battle against the mages of Oakgrove. The Shadow Bears were the last allies that stood by Oakgrove's side in the end. She had her shadows stolen from her. Her life was stolen from her before my very eyes. And…" Remy paused. "I will live without her forever. When a Shadow Bear grieves, they grieve for life. I will never ever forget my mate. Your nightmares may never leave you… But they are a part of what makes you, you child."

Her sobs quieted a little. Remy had never revealed much about his past. She could feel his pain and sorrow. She heard his whimpers at night. But he had never told her why.

"Promise you'll never leave me, Remy…" She lifted her head and Remy removed his, standing up next to her. He towered over her, standing over seven feet tall at his shoulders. It made her height of six feet seem tiny. But despite that, he wasn't so scary. He had sworn to protect her when he realized she was his ward.

"Natalia, even in death, I will always protect you even if I have to force my mother herself down here to protect you." He knelt, letting her climb up onto his back. She scratched behind his ear and laughed a little.

"You're not dying anytime soon. But that *is* a fight that would tear down the heavens."

Remy stood up, traveling back to the cottage. Natalia's mist still followed them, trailing behind like it was a wraith itself.

She supposed that was what she was supposed to be. Wraiths were undead Fae- but as far as she could tell, she had only ever been human. Whoever had taken her was trying to create a new kind of wraith. She could control mist, run as fast as a wraith, and at certain times, could turn transparent like one. From what she could tell, she was taller than she had been in her past life, and paler than it. Even her eyes were more blue than they ever had been.

It took a large amount of fear, anger, and absolutely no focus to turn fully into a wraith. But she could turn herself into a mist-like form that allowed her to go through objects if she ever had to.

Natalia shuddered- she had only ever done that once. After that... Well, she had never felt scared with Remy.

The trees whispered to each other around her, their leaves shaking with laughter.

She could almost understand them. That was something else she supposed came from being a... Wraith, if you could even call her that. She wished she could talk to them. Wisdom rolled off on the trees. They were awake but not awake.

"What do they say?" Remy murmured. She strained to listen, trying to pick out some words.

"They're saying… that a big, noisy bear is disturbing their sleep."

Remy roared with laughter, stomping his feet. "Maybe if they wake up, they can tell me themselves!"

And so they went, walking slowly through the woods, basking in the warm sun peeking through the leaves. A small breeze whirled around them as if to say hello.

Life- that was what she felt. She and Remy had never discovered if she was truly alive or just undead. Life was whirling around her and she sat there in the middle of it all.

"Thank you for telling me about your mate, Remy. I'm sorry you lost her." She whispered to him, as if the trees had ears, and this was a conversation she didn't want to share. She felt his feet falter a little, but he continued walking.

"I would do anything for you, Natalia. I will never completely understand the horrors you have gone through but… An immortal lives with their grief forever. Nothing can cure it. It never lessens. Death is the only way to heal. Until I pass, I will never see my mate. Meeting you, though, has given me purpose." Remy went silent before letting out a slow breath. "She would have loved you."

Natalia laid on his neck, scratching behind his ears again. "Do you think I would still be your ward if she was still here?"

Remy completely stopped his walking. He turned his head a little towards her and looked back forward. "Natalia, if she was still here, I believe you would be her ward. Wards… As much as I am to protect you, we heal each other. A ward and their protector are brought together because both have holes in their heart. Ameniel… She was pregnant with a cub when we went into battle. Refused to tell me. If she hadn't died, she would have lost the cub regardless. Afterwards, a healer told me it had passed before the battle. You would have healed her, and she would have protected you fiercely. Perhaps more fiercely than I. She wouldn't have just demanded Tenebris come down- she would have called upon all the Gods."

"When I die one day Remy, I'll find her." With that promise, Remy began his walk back. The forest had quieted. The sky was dark- how long had they been out here? "Remy, did I lose time? I thought I woke up rather early this morning."

Remy's voice was choked. "You did wake up early, Natalia."

She gripped his fur. "What is that?"

Remy didn't answer. Only began running away from whatever that darkness was. She could sense his fear, could sense whatever it was wasn't good. The darkness rolled upon them like thunderclouds. It buzzed with energy, alive. Tendrils reached out, trying to grab them.

"Remy, what is it?" He still didn't answer, only began running faster. "Remy, what's going on?"

Remy snarled, roaring in fury and fear. Natalia froze in shock and kept quiet. She knew the fury wasn't directed at her- she could feel it through their soul tie, the fear rippling down it. She clutched close to him and dared to look back at the darkness rolling after them. It was a dark cloud, blowing through the trees faster than any wind she had ever seen.

And it was... Calling out to her.

Not in a gentle way. It was taunting her, begging her, yelling to her.

"Remy... It wants me, not you. If I jump off, you may be able to make it." She leaned down to his ear, whispering as if the darkness couldn't hear them. But she knew that rolling storm heard those words and laughed at her.

"I will not let you go. I would die before I let you go into that alone." Remy snarled; his fury was pointed directly at her this time. Natalia paused, biting her lip. "Don't do it, Natalia. It's taunting you. Take it from a child of darkness... You would not make it out."

Natalia shut her eyes and prayed to whatever Gods still listened.

"*Natalia don't.*" Remy snarled, still running at full speed. He didn't dare look back and neither did she, but she could feel the darkness gaining on them.

"I'm sorry."

She let go of him, letting herself fly off his back. She blocked out his scream, ignored him calling for her down their soul tie. Screaming for her to come back.

The darkness laughed and laughed and *laughed*. It whirled around her and poked at the mist that surrounded her now.

It is good to see you again, Natalia.

What?

You haven't figured it out? You don't have those memories yet?

Oh, she was thoroughly confused now.

I'm sure you are.

The darkness continued to surround her, whirling around her. She couldn't pinpoint the voice, couldn't decipher where the darkness started and ended.

And her head was *pounding.*

I'm sure it is. All those memories, building up, waiting to burst out.

How could it hear her thoughts?

I remade you, Natalia. It is not hard to get into your head.

She was glad she didn't eat breakfast. She would have vomited everything up.

Those details aren't necessary.

She wanted to tell the darkness to get the hell out of her head, but she thought he would already know by now.

You're right, I do. And there's no chance that I'm leaving now that you let me in. Shall I let in the Shadow Bear that's trying to rip down the darkness surrounding us with his claws? Or shall I simply let the darkness take the life from him?

No. No no no no no *no-*

What if I took your life instead?

Yes. Anything but Remy- anything but the closest thing she had left to family. But… What was this darkness?

You really don't remember?

The pounding in her head continued building. She'd tear down the darkness herself if this thing didn't get to the gods damned point…

You were a failed experiment. After you, I perfected the experiments but… You, you were a failure that somehow escaped. I've been tracking you down ever since. You need to be eliminated.

Natalia clawed at the ground, trying to crawl out of the grasp of the darkness.

Oh, you can't escape me.

Out of the cover of the darkness came a man, hair black as night and eyes red as fire. His skin was snow white and his face was more skeletal than human. A hole hollowed its way in her chest. She remembered that face. She felt her hands melting onto those bars again-

I was an experiment once too. Unlike you, I learned to control myself.

It's a shame you weren't more useful.

His darkness lashed out as if it was another limb, gripping onto her chest, trying to claw its way into her heart.

Control- she could control it- and the darkness slipped through her. It wasn't fear that controlled her. She controlled the fear.

What?

She stood shakily, the mist extending beyond her wraithlike body like a cloak. It covered her black hair, fell to the ground, and cascaded around her. Her olive toned skin had turned to a bluish hue.

How did you resist my powers?

Natalia didn't answer. She ran forward, faster than she had before. Twirled around him like she herself was mist. Lashed out with nails like daggers, looking to grab any part of him. To tear into him.

She felt him in her mind still, panicking, looking for any way out. But she slammed down walls, locking him in. Moving those walls into a tiny spot so he only had a corner. He was spinning in real life, trying to pinpoint her. His darkness was lashing out at her and trying to grab onto her, but she was too quick.

But then… He stopped. Let her grab onto him.

He laughed, and grabbed onto those walls she had formed, dragging down dagger-like claws. She tore into whatever part of him she could with claws of her own. They fell down together, clutching onto each other.

If I can't take you down myself, I'll let you take yourself down.

And then she was plunged into herself.

She awoke on a table. She was stiff, felt like she'd fall apart the moment she moved. She struggled to open her eyes but managed to squint them open a little.

"What the hell is she doing?" Who was that? Last she remembered, she had been in the dungeons and a fire had set out over Hallenfall. The light was so bright, but she still peered out and-

Holy gods. Her skin was peeled back, revealing bones and guts and

"I thought she was still dead! She wasn't supposed to come back. What the hell happened?" She was dead? She had died and she was filleted open. Oh my god she had been filleted open-

The world spun around her, the darkness covering them both. Distantly she heard Remy's snarls, but it didn't register to her whether he was close or not. She spun in and out of consciousness, unaware of the man anymore. Only aware of her pain and confusion.

She awoke again, this time covered in ashes. She was both aware and unaware of the last time she had awoken. The thought laid in the back of her mind like a cat sleeping but always ready to pounce.

She could move- she blinked a couple times, raised her hand to test that she was whole. People murmured around her and scratched on a piece of paper. She rose out of the ashes; on the same table she had been before.

On the same table she had been filleted open on.

Oh gods- where was she? Natalia's mind raced trying to make sense of it all. Her limbs were so stiff as if she had been squished together. The people around her merely watched, including a man with fiery red eyes.

She vowed to never forget those eyes. Some part of her told herself she would need to remember them.

She jumped off the table. The people merely took a step back but...
She was behind bars. Bars like the ones in Hallenfall.

"Do you remember Hallenfall?" That man with red eyes spoke. How did he know what she was thinking about?

"Barely, but yes." In truth it was very little. She remembered being in jail after just turning seventeen. She should have been going off to meet a friend so they could celebrate, but a man had disturbed all that. She remembered her mother's cries and the pound of the gavel.

Natalia looked around at her surroundings. They seemed to be under-ground- there were no windows anywhere and it was cave-like. Not like the dragon caves that her mother had told her stories about. But a cave where people were tortured and never seen again.

Fear crept in and then- a mirror, a mirror was in the room.

Oh gods. She wasn't filleted open anymore, but she couldn't have been more than five years old.

"You'd be correct. When we gave you the elixir of fae and phoenix blood, we used our magic to control what you remembered and how old you would be when you came back to life. Since you were only a human, we were hoping the fae blood would mask your mortality. Alas, the phoenix blood was not tricked... Another failed experiment." The man paused, turning around to an assistant. He whispered, but she could still hear it. "Is your man healed?"

The assistant pulled away a paper and read something on the one behind it. "Yes, sir. He's back to full strength after she killed him." The assistant whispered. Didn't they know she could hear them?

"Send your man back out to the village. Fae are still rumored to live there. Perhaps if we find one of the true fae, we can bring the wraiths back

from legend." The man pushed the assistant towards the door, before turning back to her.

"What do you mean, send your man back? I killed him." She had felt his blood trickle down her hand. She saw the life leave his eyes. The man with the fiery eyes just laughed.

"He never died. We brought his body back and brought him back to life. He was our first successful experiment." The man with the fiery eyes shrugged as if it was old news. The memories flashed before Natalia's eyes. All she could think of was the blood on her hands, the soldiers from the village that rushed out when she screamed in shock, her skin melting onto the bars...

And this man caused it.

Anger surged within her, mingling with her fear. She eyed the people behind the bars, rage blinding her.

Something propelled her forward. Her tiny body went through the bars- some part of her mind ignored the fact she went through the bars she couldn't fit through. But the other, rational part of her mind she knew she had gone through them as if they hadn't been there in the first place.

"I thought you said the experiment failed?!" The people were scream- ing, throwing parchment and quills and ink. Glasses were knocked onto the ground and tables were flipped to slow her down.

No matter what came at her, she ran through it. Mist was curling around her and pooling beneath her feet. She grabbed a dagger and slashed at a woman's throat. Whatever guilt surrounded her when she had killed the man outside her village was gone now.

Then- the man with the fiery eyes. He was there, staring in utter amazement. She ran to stab him too, but then he grabbed her-

"People can still grab you, dear. If it is connected to life, it will be a part of your death. The mages of the West will mourn this failed experi- ment." And a dagger went deep into her gut.

Natalia let go of him, staggering back. Whirling around to find any exit. She needed to leave. She would go anywhere but here. She felt some- thing in her mind that shouldn't be there and hurriedly pushed it out with all the anger she could manage. That window- the cell mimicked her cell in Hallenfall.

So she ran as quickly as she could and leapt for the window-

Something was calling to her.

Yelling down to her.

She looked down- but there was no blood. This wasn't right. This hadn't happened.

But- this wasn't the memory.

"Natalia!" Remy was nosing her, pressing his paw on her chest, trying to get any reaction from her. She bolted up, backed a few steps away. The darkness... Was gone. And in front of her was Remy. "Don't you *ever* do that again. Do you understand?" Remy snarled, true anger showing through. But... Fear ran down that bond between them. He had been *so* scared. She had felt it.

She was almost too nervous to ask. "That man... What happened?" She leaned against a tree, which seemed to speak in a soothing manner towards her.

Remy stepped to the side a little to show her the body. "When I got here, you had already ripped his throat out with your bare hands."

"Remy... He made me remember. He gave me my memories. I don't think I was supposed to come back from those. That man called himself a mage from the West. Said I was a failed experiment."

Remy's eyes widened and he let out a pained noise. "We need to find Makani."

CHAPTER 5

A CHILD OF FIRE AND ICE

IT SHOULD HAVE BEEN EASY. ALL SHE HAD TO DO WAS GO IN front of the panel of judges and explain her daughter's case. Except, if she lost the case, the gods would decide that her daughter would die.

So, there she stood, trembling before a panel of 25 judges who would decide by the end of the speech whether her newborn would live or die. Her notecards were jumbled on the podium from accidental shuffling, and she could barely reach the microphone. One by one, the judges stared her down, impatiently waiting for her to begin.

"I stand before this honorable court in search of a pardon for my daughter, whose birth is not her fault. Only fifteen days old, my darling Artemisia knows nothing of this world. She knows nothing of her origins and only displays the slightest curiosity at our culture. She is a moldable creature who, with control and monitoring, could make a first-rate citizen and soldier that our Gods can be proud of. My lover, Archimedes, has already been killed in a war on the southern coast. Our daughter could be the binding of our Gods, should you so wish."

The Judges stared her down, each one a representative for each of their 25 Gods. These heavenly beings did not lightly invite people to their court. Diana had tried so hard to keep her daughter a secret but deep inside, she knew her daughter with all her power could not be kept hidden. When they called her to the center of the continent for her daughter's case to be pleaded to the 25 judges, Diana wept.

Now, she met each of their gazes, determined to show the ferocity in which she would fight for her daughter. One cleared his throat and jotted something on a piece of parchment before speaking.

"Archimedes was a guardian of the southern realm, ruled by fire and war. You, Diana, are a guardian of the northern realm, ruled by ice and trade. Have those traits shown up in the newborn?"

Diana glanced down; her breath caught in her throat. "Yes. Artemisia has exhibited both the water and ice molding talents of my people as well as the fire bending talents of her father. I have found that while she is sensitive to both the heat and the cold, it is nowhere near the degree of a mortal. Altogether, neither her powers nor her temperature sensitivity has proved a detriment to her development." She steeled her voice. Diana had rehearsed her answer all day and night for the past two weeks, yet even as she said the words she knew so well, she feared her answer was still wrong.

The judges shared looks, all glancing down at the newborn before them.

She poured her will and love into the infant, trying to persuade her to stay calm. One fit, and she could turn the judges into a block of ice or encase them all in a wall of fire. Diana supposed that was why the judges had chosen the center of the continent. That was where ley lines of the continent crossed- it suppressed all of their magic, rendering them near powerless.

It was the same reason Diana and Archimedes had chosen the center of the continent for Diana to give birth. It was risky, being so close to the homes of the judges... But it was worth it, knowing they were safe.

One of the judges spoke up. "Sisters and Brothers, could we not use these talents to our advantage? For years we have been fighting each other, never quite being able to unite each other. Here we have the one who could!" His voice rose in excitement, though Diana couldn't help but notice the look on his face... One that spoke of exploitation rather than true acceptance.

She knew her daughter would never be safe in either half of the realm. Diana looked down at Artemisia and saw the light of her life. Her eyes opened and gold irises stared up at her. Those eyes alone were a sign that she had been a gift from the Gods.

But a gift she could not be in either half. All these judges saw was a weapon, one that could help them dominate and control each other once and for all. That was all they cared about- how much they could control one another in a place where they had the same amount of power. A third judge spoke, bearing the same look that Diana was sure she had on her face- dismay.

"Sisters and Brothers, perhaps all this newborn will do is cause trouble for the realms. There is enough war in the kingdoms of Tarlatan. If it cannot master its powers, it would be a curse in this realm."

Diana's fear spiked.

"I implore you... This union created a newborn gifted from the gods themselves. Her golden eyes glitter with fire and ice. She could be a princess of both if you allowed her. Or she could live in solidarity with me, at the center of the ley lines, where her magic is no danger to the world." She would not let her daughter die.

The judges shared gazes before settling their stares back on her.

Twenty-Five Years Later

Artemisia brushed the dirt off of her apron before standing in the garden. Her basket was full of leafy greens, fruits, and vegetables from her and her mother's garden.

She took a deep breath and smiled before grabbing her basket. This garden... It had to be her favorite place in the world. No matter what time of year, it was full of life. Her walk back to the house took her through winding paths past some goats, sheep, and chickens. Their hunting dogs slept peacefully on the porch, enjoying the breeze and sun.

"Did you get any more strawberries today? I was thinking of making a strawberry rhubarb pie, but we used the last of the canned filling. I found the jars in someone's room..." Her mother called from the porch, rocking in her chair.

Artemisia flushed, handing the basket over to her mother. "To be fair, they had been sitting there and taunting me for so long... No, the strawberries are done for the season. I can run up to the market to see if they have any left."

Her mother shook her head, drumming her fingers against the railing on the porch. "It's strange. The growing season shouldn't be done yet. We didn't even get half the harvest we got last year." Artemisia watched her mother mull over the items in her basket. She inspected the quality of the leaves, the colors of the fruits and vegetables... And sighed. "Must be an off year. It happens every so often."

"Well, I happen to know that we still doubled the harvest that the Mayfall's got this year, so I'd say we're doing pretty good." Artemisia knelt and scratched the pup behind the ears.

Her mother laughed. "We could double the Mayfall's harvest by doing absolutely nothing. They couldn't develop a green thumb to save their lives. Come inside- we have to do some canning now that *someone* ate the jars of pie filling."

Even though her mother had dismissed it, Artemisia couldn't help but think that there were things her mother left unsaid.

They walked into the cottage together, with Artemisia flinging a small spark into the fireplace. Her mother got to work drawing the chill from some of the food and routing it into the icebox.

She wasn't sure how her mother did it- but it was fascinating every time Artemisia watched. It was as if the chill floated along the air and fell into the icebox.

For as long as Artemisia had lived here, that had been their routine. Her mother taught her how to garden and raise livestock so that they could be a team. They would start their day letting the livestock into the right fields, filling the troughs, and clearing the garden. Her mother would prepare food and Artemisia would do the maintenance around the house.

Artemisia would marvel at the way her mother pretended this magic was nothing but life, and that her fires were something to avoid. Her mother would chastise her for relying on her magic.

Day in, day out, everything remained the same. They repaired the same spots in their clothes, collected wood from the same part of the forest, and never went further than the one market.

One might expect Artemisia to be bored. And for the most part... She was, but she could be content living with her mother. Her mother told her all the stories of the continent, from the highest towers of Luce Stellarum to the deepest depths of the Corinthian Ocean.

Gods, she wished to walk those streets and slip onto the beach, so that she might just dip her toes into the ocean. Or perhaps she would travel to one of the safeguards of the Guardians of the Realms so that she and her mother might learn more about their magic.

They practiced their magic a little throughout the day on tasks that required it and no more. Even that remained the same and, no matter how many times Artemisia asked, her mother insisted that their magic started and ended in what could fit in the palm of their hands. Artemisia paused the sweeping and stared at the fire she had started, imagining it growing just a little more. She stared into those depths, letting it sweep her away.

It warmed her soul, the release.

"Artemisia!" Her mother shouted her name over the boiling kettle, and she snapped out of the reverie. She let out a breath, focusing it on the fire to cool it.

Artemisia checked to see if she had worn through her power and-

"I'm sorry Mother. It won't happen again." It couldn't happen again today. There was nothing left in her soul that she could reach. Her mother sighed, rubbing her temples.

"Artemisia, you say this every day. It cannot happen again. The more you rely on your magic or lean into it, the more attention it brings us." Her mother paused, looking at Artemisia. "I know you want to practice more. But I promise you- we were not gifted with more than we have."

Artemisia leaned the broom against the wall. "But mother- you've told me stories. Stories of our people who could swim in their magic, they have so much of it. If we could journey to visit them, perhaps they can see if we have more." She had never suggested it before- her mother had always moved the conversation away.

But today was different. The wind blew differently. It was as if something rippled in the air.

So, Artemisia stood her ground this time.

"Artemisia, this is our home. If we leave, who will take care of our garden and our animals while we are gone?"

"What if we did not have to come back? What if our home was somewhere else?"

Her mother stared her down hard. "Our home is nowhere but here. Now get back to work." For a moment, Artemisia almost listened as she watched her mother turn back around. But that ripple filled her soul with an energy she had never felt before.

"No, Mother. My home is with you- it doesn't matter where in the world we are. Why won't you leave?" There was something that her mother wasn't telling her. Her mother set down the knife that she had grabbed to cut up carrots and began to speak.

"Artemisia, there are things much bigger than you and I. If I told you half of the things that led to us, you would think I was insane." Her mother stopped, as if waiting for an argument. But Artemisia had none. Pain flitted in her heart. This went so much deeper than Artemisia had even thought. She could almost see the pain drifting off her mother.

Artemisia walked up to her, placing both hands on her mother's shoulders. "You are my home. You have been my mother, tutor, friend, and advisor. Even the people in the tiny market avoid us. I feel their stares, as if we are tainted. Yet, we live no differently than them. Help me understand. I cannot live with lies anymore." She placed her forehead against her mother's.

They had always done it when she was young. It was a source of comfort when tensions rose and Artemisia did not know how to calm down.

Her mother laughed. "Who is the advisor now? Take a seat on the couch." Her mother led them over before starting again. "Long ago, the Gods created this magical world. They created Tarlatan, the continent we live on and its islands, as a home for their children. It was separated into two halves- the Southern Realm and the Northern Realm. Deeply embedded into the continent are ley lines, where all magic flows through. Ley lines, Artemisia, run the world. The closer you are to the center, the more you are suppressed. The Gods created the ley lines and chose the center as the home for their judges so that their holy representatives would always remain safe against the most violent of magic users. There is a circle around the center that suppresses almost all magic. The moment you step over that ley line, is the moment that your magic is your own again."

Her mother twisted her fingers, forming a small model of the continent of Tarlatan. It was not detailed beyond mountains and rivers but glowing in the center was them. Artemisia had never seen her mother use magic so freely- and wondered how much more she had.

"The Gods created guardians for their judges. Guarding the Southern Realm were fire golems. Fire lit their souls. Guarding the Northern Realm were ice golems. Ice froze their souls. And for some time, these guardians lived in peace and hiding amongst the people of Tarlatan. They embraced a mortal appearance to not scare the people. But as the years went on, the Southern and Northern guardians found themselves locked in a civil war against each other. The Northern Guardians, you see, wanted to live in peace as tradesmen. The Southern Guardians were true warriors who could not stand the Northern Guardians dismissing their duties. The judges let the Guardians sort it out amongst themselves. I have told you all this before, of course. These are the stories of our past. But, I have not told you all the stories of our people."

Tears brimmed at her mother's eyes.

"Thirty years ago, a Northern Guardian and Southern Guardian met in war. They were powerful beings, evenly matched in every way. Every time they met, they grew closer and closer, forgetting they were enemies at times. And from their union… Grew you."

Artemisia's breath caught.

"You were never supposed to exist, to the Northern and Southern Realms. In truth, Artemisia, I don't know the full depth of your power. It was luck of the draw that the judges let you live. But I knew you were a gift from the gods. You bear the golden eyes of-"

Her mother couldn't finish her sentence before the rippling that flitted on the air rushed through their house, filling them with energy. Her magic soared to new heights- new, dizzying heights that Artemisia had never felt before. The cottage rattled with it.

Her mother- oh gods, her mother. Her once brown hair had turned silver and her eyes a bright blue. Frost tipped her fingers.

And Artemisia?

She burst off the couch to look in the mirror, expecting to see herself in at least a similar form.

But instead, golden eyes stared back. Pitch black hair replaced the dull brown that had always resembled her mother's. Fire and frost tipped her fingers.

"Mother?" She turned back, finding her mother back to normal but Artemisia remained the same. Fear sank deep in her stomach. Her own mother clutched the arm of the couch, hands shaking. "Mother?" The hunting dogs were outside barking like mad, scratching at the door.

"Artemisia… Run."

What was her mother scared of?

Artemisia didn't wait for an answer. She burst out the door and practically flew down the steps, flinging her hands out. Trying to get that frost and flame off. It froze the ground and set bushes ablaze instead, only causing Artemisia's fear to grow. She shouldn't have any more magic. She had used it all…

Behind her, the dogs ran inside, still barking like mad.

"Get off of me!" She screamed it but screaming only

caused the frost to spread and fires to grow higher. If her mother was following her, she didn't know. Gods, what was happening?

Behind her branches snapped, as if something was indeed chasing her. But every time she turned around, there was no one there. Her mother would have sent the hunting dogs off after her by now if it was her.

No, her soul told her this was something much, much worse.

Her heart raced. She had to get away from the house- she knew her mother could put out the fires, but she had to run, far *far away*.

Was her mother still alive to put out the fires? Had whatever been chasing her gotten to her mother, too?

The further she ran, the more energy swirled inside of her. It was like it was going to burst out of her. Artemisia fell to her knees, clutching her head in her hands.

Gods, she felt like she was going to explode.

Deep inside her, something was telling her to calm down- to take deep breaths, and that it would all be okay, but the pain practically kicked the voice out of her body. She buried herself beneath the magic, hoping that the pain would go away.

Well, at least today is different, Artemisia grimly thought.

And for one moment, the pain flicked as she rocked back and forth. Like something was trying to emerge but she was too close and yet too far.

It had been getting worse the further and further she ran from the house and-

Ley lines, Artemisia, run the world. The closer you are to the center, the more you are suppressed. The Gods created the ley lines and chose the center as the home for their judges so that their holy representatives would always remain safe against the most violent of magic users. There is a circle around the center that suppresses almost all magic. The moment you step over that ley line, is the moment that your magic is your own again.

Gods, Artemisia thought, letting a pained breath loose. She had thought that was just a part of a story her mother had told her. But... But maybe, those hadn't just been stories. Maybe there had been ley lines that had been created by gods...

She looked up and saw a river overhead. It was a branch of a river that would reconverge further downstream and... formed a near perfect circle with the branches in doing so.

Artemisia barreled further into herself, trying to ignore the pain as she stepped back up and sprinted even further. The flames around her grew, one side hot and one side cold. She approached the river faster and faster and without thinking, she leapt.

Fear had creeped inside of her, but even when she thought that she would fall, a wind carried her over the river and an explosion of power pushed her to the other edge as she crossed the middle.

Artemisia hadn't even landed before the flames engulfed her. One side was a blazing orange and the other one was an ice blue. Wings of flame replaced arms and her legs were talons. Another one of her mother's stories came back to her.

Phoenixes once roamed this earth. It was said that they were a symbol of a gift from the Gods, but as people forgot the Gods, they burned out. Ashes that should have held a phoenix reborn crumbled to dust. It is said that one day, a phoenix will return when needed most, as a reminder that the gods never forgot their creatures.

She let out a sharp cry, testing her wings of flame. In her soul, what was once a drop of magic that could fit into her palm, was a pool of magic that never ended.

The ripple was stronger now more than ever. It was like an echoing from a beacon.

Artemisia flew towards it.

She flew and flew, going over mountains and towns and rivers and valleys. She flew until she found a stone castle with people fleeing. Thunderclouds brewed overhead, and lighting bristled.

She peered down at the ground, and let the magic turn her to ash so she might be reborn back into her human form on the ground.

Two Months Later…

Artemisia settled in at her desk in the mountains. Two long months had passed. She had collected herself and journeyed as far away from the center as she could.

She had received word from her mother just yesterday- and now she stared down at the envelope. The ink seal was pressed with her mother's sigil of the Northern Realm and the lavender that grew in the garden.

Her heart lurched at the memories and everything she had left behind.

She pushed it aside and peeled off the seal, gently opening the envelope, and pulling out the letter.

"Dear Artemisia,

I hope you have found safety. The judges have condemned me to stay in the center of the continent until you return. And in truth… I hope you never do. But a small, selfish part of me wishes you would return so I could know you are safe.

You will have so many more questions that I am unable to answer. I hope wherever this letter has found you, that the owl has done his job. Please give him a mouse and he will return.

Artemisia had already thought of that. She was just about to toss the mouse to him before reading-

Do not give him the mouse until you've put the envelope in the pouch on his talons. The greedy owl will leave before you have the chance.

Artemisia drew her hand back, eyeing the owl, who stared down the mouse.

Please let me know you are safe and promise you will not just survive, but live. I can feel something brewing. That day, whatever wave of magic that revealed our true selves even at the center of the continent, is just the beginning. I fear it will only get worse from here.

I love you, dear. You were always my home, too.

Artemisia choked on a sob, holding the parchment close to her chest. Oh, if only her mother knew the half of it. But she could not promise something that she had already given away.

Somehow, she pulled herself together.

She pulled out the parchment, and grabbed a quill, dabbing against another piece of parchment to rid it of the excess ink.

"Dear Mother..."

No, she scrapped that.

"I'm not sure if I will survive. But I cannot

lie in waiting as the rest of the world crumbles around us. You sacrificed your safety for mine, and now I must sacrifice my own for yours. I cannot promise I will come home... But I can promise you, I will live."

CHAPTER 6

THE ONES WHO WERE FORGOTTEN

THERE WAS A WHISPER IN THE WIND. THE LEAVES SHIVERED AND fell to the ground.

It wasn't harsh words that the wind whispered, but the leaves were so fragile, that the cold and biting words broke them.

The whisper continued, speaking its words, and continuing down the trail. Its words weaved through the trees and fur of the animals, spooking them further away. And then there was the girl.

She was young, all by herself, with a quivering lip and one arm cuddled against her chest. Dried spots of blood stained her sleeve. She was walking slowly, through the wind and down the trail. She walked past the wind as if she was ignoring its words.

The girl was afraid, but not of the words. No, it was something entirely different...

The wind picked up, tried to shout at the girl, but all it did was howl and scare the leaves away. The girl did nothing but stop and shiver for a moment, before putting her head down and walking forward.

There was a distant shouting, that the girl seemed to respond to. She turned around, away from the wind. Began running away from something... Someone. And the wind could only whisper,

'Where do you go, child? Why now do you run?'

And the child suddenly halted to a stop, her little lip quivering with contemplation and confusion. The voice yelling only grew stronger, louder. The wind carried on, surrounding the child, and coaxing her for some sort of answer. And the child just looked more lost, until something caught her eye. A little doe, just standing there, as the leaves fell around them. The yelling still grew louder. But the girl was entirely focused on the little doe approaching her slowly, until it was just close enough for the girl to brush her fingers against the rough fur.

Pure awe struck away any fear, contemplation, and confusion. For a moment, it was only them two. Just the little girl and the little doe, both reflections of one another. Both scared little creatures, trying to find their way in the world. Neither afraid of the wind, nor the incessant yelling that continued through the tender moment.

And then the wind tried to stop the yelling, by shouting its own words.

The little doe was spooked away.

And then there was a man bounding through the woods, snapping twigs, and breaking branches. The man was doing far more damage than the wind could ever have achieved, by just being there. He was not meant to be there- but the little girl, the wind couldn't tell what she was. The little girl looked up in complete terror and began running herself. Tears streamed down her face, like the river that roared not a mile away. There was a strange wet patch on the little girl's leggings, that the wind couldn't identify at first.

And when the scent fell upon the wind, it roared in fury.

Roared up to the gods, wondering if any would come down to help. He was too far, but perhaps one of them could help-

The wind's sisters and brothers seemed to ignore his pleas. As if they glanced up and looked away, continuing whatever they were doing. Ignored the wind whenever it carries the cries of the little girl and the taunts of the man past their ears. *Laughed it off,* in some cases.

So, he ran as fast as he could, letting his wind carry him. He jumped into the air and caught a current, spilling and flipping. His immortal heart was beating faster and faster, worry creeping into his heart. Even his wind couldn't carry him there fast enough, he would be too late... A cry crept out louder and he heard a large crash.

He sent his wind roaring down, the trees holding on for dear life. He heard some of the older trees waking from a slumber, grumbling in annoyance- but the younger ones were urging him on, warning him to continue, warning him that he needed to *fly faster.* The wind told him he wasn't too far now, just another couple miles, perhaps he could make it...

Another thundering answered his wind, coupling together. The forest filled with darkness, and he wondered idly if one of his brethren had joined him but... No, not one of his siblings, but one of their children. The thundering footsteps were filled with an equal impatience and worry. A feral grin fell upon his face, and he thought to himself, *there are some things that should not have been forgotten.*

They fell upon the man like a wild tornado, sending him flying. A breeze caressed the girl, catching her on a current and gently placing her down before she could be sent flying. Around her, he placed a whirling sphere of air that no one could penetrate. And when he was certain the little girl was safe, he turned around with the Shadow Bear stalking the man down at his side. He scented the anger on the man. No twinge of fear, but instead anger that his quarry had been taken from him. The wind roared past him and the Shadow Bear, focusing its might on the man. The man tumbled back, desperately trying to grab onto trees and branches.

One tree shouted with indignation at the man who treated it in such a way as he tried to escape his treatment and let the root he grabbed onto loosen so he might fall off.

Another breeze carried the scent of fear now. "Who in the gods are you two?" The man was screaming, pleading unintelligibly. He knelt in front of the man, the Shadow Bear still standing next to him. He lifted a finger and the wind came roaring past. Lowered the finger and the wind slowed to a gentle breeze. Horror and realization fell upon his face as the wind circled around his throat, tightening more and more... "No, no it can't be..." The man managed to squeak out.

The man turned over to the Shadow Bear, inclining his head. "Would you like the honor?" The Shadow Bear grinned- if a bear could grin- and leapt in the air, snarling and latching his jaws around the man's head. A squeak aired behind them- the little girl, who had jumped in surprise within her cocoon of swirling air.

The Shadow Bear spit the head out in disgust, kicking his feet back as he turned around.

"Thank you for your assistance, Makani. It will be a debt never forgotten." The Shadow Bear inclined his head towards him, before turning his head back towards the child. "Do you know who this child is?"

Makani shrugged, idly letting the wind sweep the body away on a current. It would be dumped far from here, where only scavengers would find it. "My wind reported it to me, carrying the sounds along the currents. I ordered it to try and save the child while I ran there, but no one speaks our ancient tongue anymore." Makani paused, thinking to himself. "The Shadow Bears are the children of my sister, Tenebris. What is your name? I've been trying to figure out which of her children you are but cannot remember. It's been... so very long since I've talked with Tenebris."

"My name is Remy. I am the youngest of my mother's children. She will not be happy that I interfered in the business of mortals but... I locked eyes with the child while running over to see what was going on. I believe... I believe she is my ward." Remy and Makani strolled up to the little girl, slowing the cocoon of wind enough that she could leave if she wished, but still felt protected against them if she was scared.

"Well met, Remy. If it is any consolation, the gods have not paid attention to this world in a long while. She has no hold over you." Makani knew it was no consolation. He had met many of his sibling's children. Some wanted nothing to do with their parents. Others couldn't care one way or the other. And the ones like Remy who feared their parents... They would live in seclusion until Makani drew them out, convincing them to live their life to the fullest.

The girl stepped out of the cocoon and for the first time, Makani got a proper look at her.

The little girl's scent was different, Makani noted. Something not entirely human. Something not entirely... Alive. That little bit of her that wasn't human must have understood what Remy was- what Makani was- and launched herself at Remy, clutching his fur in her fingers as she sobbed.

That was when Makani felt it on his wind, calling to him. Anger, malice, and betrayal. It was a message from the gods, calling him to their grand palace in the sky. He let his wind lift him up on currents, falling into it- letting his old bones relax. Makani had known what sending those sounds past the ears of his siblings would cause. It would anger them to know that he had interfered with mortals, the last creation by their father that he left to them to watch over.

Watch over, they said, and nothing more. They were children angry with their father and would take it out on his beloved creation, even if it meant being petty.

It hurt Makani to no end to leave mankind to their own devices. To watch them kill each other, manipulate each other, starve, die from disease so easily preventable... Every so often he intervened. But today... Today was the first time he had shown his siblings what was truly going on with mortals. He couldn't take it anymore. He couldn't hide in the deserts of Rubicon, letting the sand dunes reflect the noises off somewhere else.

These mortals- they loved their gods. They loved gods who couldn't care about them less, and Makani hated his siblings for it. They made different names for them, built temples in their honor, and prayed to them. Some worshipped all the gods, some worshipped one. Some mortals even worshipped their father and mother, despite the fact that their father and mother were long dead. That was why Makani loved living amongst the mortals... They loved their gods without even knowing if they still existed. They believed in the gods even when they shouldn't. A few mortals even worshipped him and gave him different names. He heard their prayers on the wind every so often and smelt the burning incense that drifted along the sand dunes.

So up, up, up his wind carried him, past clouds and mountains, up into the never-ending sky. As the world turned to night, he turned over to look over the world. He stared below at the little lights from lanterns in the middle continent of Tarlatan and the faelights in the east. To the west, darkness brewed.

Curiosity struck him and he sent winds down to investigate, to see why it might be so dark. Makani did not often come up this high. And, come to think of it, he could not remember feeling winds in the west. As if walls had been put up, covering the continent.

Then Makani choked for air, falling a few feet before he pulled his winds back. His lungs heaved for air, and he forced the winds to push him higher as he stared in horror at that western continent. It was still dark, completely black. His winds had gone to the continent, but the moment they touched any leaf or building they had been stolen from him like life from a mortal. His heart was pounding- his wind cocooned around him, whispering of darkness and evil. Makani shook hard, prayed for his wind to carry him higher than it had in a long time, until he landed at the gates to their palace.

With his two feet planted firmly on the sacred ground, he turned to the gate, admiring it. His mother and father had built this castle with the energy of her births. The first birth created this place above all that existed. The second created the world below, where the creatures both immortal and mortal would live. The third created the buildings in the never-ending sky. The fourth created the ley lines in the Tarlatan. His mother and father knew the magic that would exist in the world below would need a conduit. So, the ley lines formed conduits to tunnel magic so that magic users below would be able to handle it. The fifth and six births created the Northern and Southern Guardians, protectors of the realm. When the gods could not protect the life below, the Guardians would step in.

The following sixteen births created the worlds below- the rivers, mountains- everything, except for the mortals, was created by the energy and magic that flowed from the births. The children grew happily in their palace, and one final birth created the gate that would protect the gods. This gate was made from magic imbued metal, unbreakable. Only the god of the forge, Hessian, could create or destroy the metal. It never varnished and, as Makani brushed his hand against it, almost pulsed with energy. He pulled away, moving his eyes down to the lock.

Makani snorted. *Of course* they locked it. Perhaps they

wanted to test to see if he still remembered how the lock opened. He gathered wind behind him, spearing it into the lock before him. He felt it compress and widen as needed around the pins, letting them all click into place. Makani pricked his finger with the dagger at his side and...

He paused for a moment, wondering if he entered, if he would ever be able to leave.

But he would not fear his siblings and let the blood drip onto the lock and slide into the opening.

Slowly the lock clicked one more time, before the gates slid open and revealed the paradise beyond. Buildings of marble, metal, and wood interlaced together forming a main courtyard. Beyond, mountains jutted further into the never-ending sky. Each mountain and hill in this land was home to a soul, which could be seen from the world below in what mortals called stars. There the soul slumbered, resting for all eternity.

"So, I see you remembered how to open the lock." Makani turned around, seeing his sister Tenebris stalk out of the shadows.

"I could never forget. I just never wanted to come back after what happened." Makani stared his sister down, letting his wind cocoon around him like a second skin. His brothers and sisters possessed multitudes of magic. He would be an idiot to not walk in protected.

Tenebris scowled at him before motioning him forward, towards the amphitheater. "Our siblings are waiting." Makani bristled but walked with her towards the amphitheater, where his 21 other siblings awaited. Power practically rolled off the amphitheater and, for a moment, Makani's heart stopped. He had forgotten what it was like to be around all this power.

"Brother. You've kept us waiting." Tristique, his eldest brother, rumbled from his chair in the middle. Tenebris took her spot in the amphitheater, next to where Makani's spot used to be. At the very top sat two empty chairs... One for their mother and one for their father.

Makani refused to sit, preferring to keep his back to the door for an easy escape. "I didn't realize there had been a time set. I never got words, just anger." He eyed each of his siblings, not daring to back down.

His sister, Alexandra, let the fiery crown on her head flare. "You should have never left in the first place. There is a reason you received only anger." Their brother, Aquetious, soothed her flames with water, only earning a breath of fire that caused him to steam. Aquetious curled his lip and pulled his hand away. His twin, Alesia, sent some of her saltwater over to cool the areas that had steamed.

"Siblings, that day has come and gone. We need to focus on the issue at hand." Tristique sent a rumble throughout the lands, reminding them exactly why they had gathered here. Makani's wind steadied him against the rumble, keeping him mercifully upright. Tristique focused his heavy gaze upon Makani. "When Mother and Father passed, we voted to not interfere with the mortals or their lands. Our magic would live in the world of its own accord, flowing through the ley lines of Tarlatan. It needs no more magic, after Mother and Father gave it enough to last a lifetime. And yet, you, Makani, decided you would interfere with mortal business."

"Brother, you forget I was not at that vote. When you voted, I left this place and you sealed the gate behind me, telling me to never return. I've lived amongst the mortals this entire time, yet you've never said anything. Why now? Why has Tenebris' child, one of the Shadow Bears, not been called with me today?" Makani paced forward, each word a jab of wind speared at his siblings.

Tenebris' shadows lashed out and grabbed the spears of wind, forcing them back towards Makani. "I have not spoken to my children in eons. Just like the other children of the gods, my children are facets of my magic, living in the world below of their own accord. Whether they live or die is no concern of mine, just as their actions do not reflect my own views. Do not bring them up to disguise your own misfortune." A thinly veiled threat- Makani tightened the cocoon around him.

"You lived as a hermit amongst the mortals. You gave us no reason to interfere. The immortals, our children, of the world below protect it well enough with the help of the Guardians. There is no need for our interference." Alesia's pale lips pursed together. Her skin was almost translucent- it was not often that she came out of the oceans of the never-ending sky and to see him was almost jarring.

Alexandra hissed, gripping the edge of her seat so hard it scorched. "We should have interfered with you, Makani, long before now. Why do you have these sentiments for these mortals? Father created them and with that, killed him and Mother. If it was not for those mortals, we could have lived in peace. No- he needed to make one final creation that would use so much magic it would kill them." The flames of her fiery crown soared even higher- so high, that Makani's wind grew scared and flew around the flames, smothering them down.

"Alexandra, these mortals did not ask to be made. A part of Mother and Father live on in them. Some of them can use magic and are not immortal. Some of them worship you. Some of them even have connections with you that, if you would pay attention, you would have noticed. How can you dismiss them so easily? Mother and Father both knew the cost. Mother and Father died, letting their magic soak into the earth, so that when the mortal's pass away, their souls could join the souls of the immortals here. And the living mortals, despite their grief, could continue to live on and would heal. Mother never wanted them to live with the pain she would have to live with eternally. Why should I hate them for something so beautiful?" It was something Makani sometimes wished to experience. Not death- but loving something so much that you could grieve it. As an immortal, Makani could create his children. It would take little bits of magic he could never regain and, sometimes, he could combine magic with one of his siblings to create a child.

But those children would always be immortal. He would never mourn their loss, as they so rarely died except for battle and heartbreak.

His sister Fauna and her twin Flora joined hands and walked down towards him. Their siblings all paused with tension floating through the air so thick, even his brother, Hessian, could not cut through it. "We understand your love, Makani. Our triplet was lost and so the beings below, the animals and plants, became mortal. An unexpected twist of events. It was not the magic of birth, but the magic of death that created their mortality. Mother did not want them to live with that pain. We feel our triplet's soul in those beings below, despite her not being here. Father designed mankind specifically- had it in mind from the beginning. Our very forms are in the shape of mankind. Yet our siblings forget this." Alexandra roared, flame blasting from her mouth. Tenebris bristled with shadows blasting out. Tristique, meanwhile, watched in curiosity.

"Our littlest brother, causing strife unheard of amongst the gods. Makani, you never cease to surprise me." Tristique smiled a little, tapping his fingers against the arm of his chair.

Makani felt Fauna and Flora join him on either side. With the support of two of his siblings, Makani spoke with renewed confidence. "Brother, there is something evil coming to the world below. I cannot stand by and wait any longer. That girl- she is mortal, but something else lives within her. And the western continent lives in darkness. It is as if no life is on that continent. I sent my winds to investigate and the moment my wind touched any surface, it was stolen from me. When was the last time any of us had any contact with the western continent?"

Whispers rumbled amongst his siblings and Tristique raised an eyebrow. Thoros broke his silence, speaking above the whispers. "I have had contact with only one. They live on the western continent. It is as if the continents are two separate worlds. Something has cleaved them from the rest of the world and darkens it from our view."

"What, exactly, would you wish us to do, Makani?" Hessian spoke, his words cutting through his wind like steel.

"I am not asking for aid to help the mortals, nor am I so foolish to expect any of you to descend from the never-ending sky to help the mortals. All I ask is that you let me leave in peace and do not interfere with my work." Makani sent a prayer out on the wind to his Mother and Father. He did not know if they were still out there, but if Fauna and Flora could feel the soul of their triplet... Maybe Mother and Father's souls were out there too.

Grumbling amongst his siblings ensued, but to his shock it was Tenebris who spoke. "I vote to let Makani leave in peace. It is clear he will not stay. We do not know what the death of a god will do to the world below. It would be an insult to Mother to kill him." Fauna, Flora, and Thoros echoed her vote and the rest of the gods eyed Tristique, Makani included.

He paused, as if mulling over the words placed before him. "Makani shall be allowed to leave as he was once before. Our littlest brother has always had more of a heart than the rest of us. If he feels he can help, then we shall let him. I will not stop you and nor shall any other god stop you." Tristique let the unspoken words fall to the wind, so that only he could hear.

Our siblings may bear hatred for the mortals below, but I do not. Our siblings are a violent, vengeful bunch. Fauna and Flora are only spared because of the loss they faced. I must stay neutral to appease our siblings, but know I will always be watching over.

Makani nodded slightly, ignoring the tears that pricked at his eyes. He turned to leave, but Fauna and Flora grabbed his wrists. "We cannot go with you because our home is here. We do not know the pain we will feel to be amongst the mortals with our sister's soul living within their own. But if you should find yourself in battle needing us, call for us. We will answer despite the pain we would feel." Fauna and Flora pulled him close, embracing him. He stiffened- it had been so, so long since they had done this, any of them. He couldn't remember the last time they had hugged.

So, Makani embraced them back, remembering Fauna's tawny eyes and the greenish hue to Flora's skin.

He didn't remember the descent down, only remembering that he commanded his wind to carry him home to the dunes. It had been so long since he had seen his siblings and without them, a part of his soul ached. Mother and Father had never wanted them to apart. When they called their children to a meeting to let them know what would happen, they asked for them to not only watch over the world, but to stay together. To not let their loss tear them apart. Makani had tried so hard- but when his siblings became so vengeful, he had to leave. It was the only choice he had to be able to watch over the mortals.

In truth, he didn't understand his sibling's hatred. It had been a decision Mother and Father made together. But Mother's children looked so much like mankind and when she saw parents mourning their children below, she wished to give them some sort of peace. The ability to heal, as she would never be able to from her own loss. Makani supposed that his siblings thought if their father had never created mankind, that Mother would never have felt so inclined to sacrifice herself and Father for them.

Makani landed safely on the ground, facing his own home in the sand dunes. It was tucked between two dunes, winds constantly whirling throughout the house and around the outside to ensure that the endless sand stayed out of his house. He stared at the dunes, positioned so perfectly so that Makani wouldn't hear the prayers to him.

And his magic lashed out, wind whirling fast, sand flying everywhere. He whirled the sand, depositing it across the landscape, until his house was on top of a dune rather than between two. Prayers floated around the air, and he answered, sending wind to them. Sending candles flickering higher than ever before and whirling around heads. For the first time, Makani felt his soul come to life in a way it never had before. He felt the magic surge beneath him in the ley lines, felt the souls of the mortals who had connections with him and...

Makani fell to his knees. He felt his mother and father's soul surging beneath him in those ley lines, their magic imbued into the very core of the world. He choked back a sob, covering his mouth. He had always hidden himself from the world. He hid his true self so that no one would recognize his power, blocked out the prayers of those who would try to reach him... All because he was caught between his soul and a feud with his siblings.

But Makani was free of that burden and could truly live, for the first time in his immortal life.

He looked at the landscape around him, and let a little tornado settle beneath him as he sat and thought.

There were so many mortals who could use magic. He may control wind, but he could react to any magic. While he might not be able to use it, the raw magic of his mother and father running through his veins gave him an innate understanding of all magic. And with the evil coming...

Mortals trained to be able to use their magic... That could be useful... Makani mused, rolling around on his tornado. Mortals who had a connection with his mother and father gained the ability to use certain types of magic. Water, fire, healing, earth, wind... Elemental magic. Some mortals who had a higher connection and worshipped his mother and father gained rarer types of magic, but those had been lost to time itself.

Makani would not let time stop him now, however.

Over the next decade, Makani set about building a school in the desert of Rubicon. He met with the King of Corsair who ruled over the Rubicon Desert and even recruited healers straight from the King himself. The King, who was so joyous that a god had chosen his kingdom to settle in, financed the school and even proclaimed Makani the highest god in their religion.

Tristique would have a fit over that, Makani snorted. But the King could not be persuaded to budge.

Mortals soon came from all over Tarlatan proclaiming to have magic. Some did and some did not. The ones who did not, Makani paid for entry to a university or apprenticeship in the kingdom of their choosing and were sent off with a bag of gold for any other expenses. If he could not help them learn magic, he would help them get an education or to learn a trade.

Occasionally, he would risk sending a breeze over to the western continent. The moment he felt that stifling darkness, he pulled away. It had been years since his curiosity had first sparked and he sent that wind before he confronted his siblings. Nothing had changed since- the continent had only grown more and more stifling. Death almost instantly hit his nose whenever he sent a breeze in. Makani often wondered if he should call down his sisters and force the western continent into battle, but in his bones, he knew it was not the right time.

Should he and his sisters fall, unknown chaos might wreak havoc upon the world. When his parents died, they had willingly done so and imbued their magic into the earth. If him and his sisters were to be murdered... He was not sure what would happen to their magic. What would happen to the animals and plants and wind that the magic of their births had originally created, and still lived on in their souls. He was not sure what his siblings would do and for that... Makani would wait. He had lived for eons already and could wait a few more years.

And then, a curious little mortal happened upon his doorstep.

The little boy couldn't have been more than ten years old, yet he carried himself like he had been around for at least twice that. He walked with a swagger that Makani should have never seen on a ten year old boy and for a moment, Makani could only blink.

"May I ask who sent you to my school?" Makani inquired, settling behind his desk. His wind swirled around the boy and-his interest peaked. Something ancient, something like his father- lay within his soul. Something Makani hadn't seen in a long time.

The boy looked around, as if he couldn't be less impressed. "I came here on my own. The markets in Corsair are brimming with talk of your school and turns out, someone who looks like a nine-year-old is easily stowed away in a cart." Something about the boy grated on his nerves, but Makani let his magic settle around his soul and curl up like a cat taking a nap.

Makani let his own silver eyes stare deep into the boy's eyes, pinning him to his spot. The boy lost a little swagger and put his hands in his lap.

"My parents were killed trying to protect me. I have this... Ability. People can ask me a question and, not only can I tell if they're lying, but I can find the answer to their question. Assassins from different courts all over the world tried to get me- so my parents smuggled me out of our village. My parents were trying to get me to your school- but the King of Corsair killed them. It took me a few years, but I figured that if I wasn't safe with a god, there was nowhere I was safe. And the worst.... I don't grow as quickly as everyone else. Boys my age are so much bigger and stronger and me... I'm eighteen-years-old and yet I look half that."

Makani smiled a little, finally understanding. He saw past the swagger and saw a boy who had his whole world flipped upside down and didn't know what to do. "When my mother and father died, certain mortals were closer to them. They worshipped them more, I suppose. Those mortals received parts of their magic upon the deaths of my parents and passed that magic onto their children. It went on for generations. Typically, nothing more than elemental magic was received from my parents. But you... Your ancestors received a gift from both my mother and father. From my mother, you received a longer life. Her magic, among many other things, was time. She could slow life or quicken it. It was not able to be done on a large scale, but for individuals here and there, she could do so. My father was a man of justice. He could seek out the truth when any of us asked him a question. Why is the sky so blue, why is the grass so green, why are the stars so bright..." Makani smiled at the memories of them laying on a hill on the earth below their never-ending sky, staring up at their home. One of the last times all of his siblings and their parents had been together.

"But my parents aren't magical. Why am I?" The boy frowned.

"Unfortunately, as time went on, your bloodlines became diluted with mortals who had no magic. By those certain families having children with families who did not receive magic, it caused it to become either dormant or skip a generation. For the generations who did have magic, it could be very little or it could be an immense amount. You received an immense amount from both your mother and your father's side. You seem to have about double the life a normal man does, and you did retain my father's truth seeking ability." The boy frowned again at Makani's words and for a moment, his face became unreadable.

The boy opened his mouth and closed it again. "I have nowhere to go." The boy lost all his swagger in an instant, unable to meet Makani's eyes. For one split second, Makani was young again, listening to his parents explain their own death. What it would mean for the world. He wanted to scream at his mother, tell her the mortals could suffer if it meant he didn't have to lose her.

For a split second, he was that boy, yelling at his parents that he would rather be gone than have them die for him. And that unreadable face suddenly gave everything away.

"You will always be welcome at my school. But if you are going to go here, you have to understand that this school will not take away your magic. You will always have your long life and your truth seeking. It will always put you in danger." Makani spoke softly. The boy looked up at him and nodded furiously.

CHAPTER 7

SEEKING THE TRUTH

THERE STOOD A BOY IN A CLEARING, WITH HIS MOTHER AND father on either side. They were pushing him behind them, staring down the soldiers of Corsair who had come to collect him.

"Sir, the boy will be safe with the King. We'd be happy to let you live if you give up the boy." The soldier held out his sword. "You don't want to make me do this." Barion whimpered behind his parents. No, he didn't want that man to do whatever he was going to do with that sword. Barion was only fifteen years old, and knew he looked about half that. His mother knelt to him and gripped his shoulders tight.

Her face crumpled as she looked him in the eyes. "Barion, you've gotta promise me that you'll continue. When we yell to run, you must run. Don't let them get you." Her mother whispered softly, kissing his cheek. His father looked down at them before looking back towards the soldiers.

"The boy won't be safe with your king. Your king will lock our son in a dungeon or in the top of a tower so no other kingdom can claim him. He'll be up there for the rest of his life. What kind of life is that?" His father gripped the sword at his side. Barion looked at his mother with panicked eyes before looking back at his father, who was unsheathing the sword.

That sword never left its sheath. It was more for show than anything- enough to scare people off who might come by with curiosity. His mother stood, pulling the knife she had always kept sheathed at her side.

"No, we can run together. We've done it this long. Please. Mother, Father, don't leave me. I can't do this on my own." His parents weren't looking back at him though, only forward. He was crying a little, begging his parents not to do this. They wouldn't survive. He couldn't survive without them. Without them… Barion had nothing.

His mother finally turned her head, enough so that Barion knew she was talking to him. "Run, son. *Run!*" She screamed as loud as she could, and his parents ran towards the men. Barion's feet obeyed her command despite him desperately wanting to stay behind. He didn't look back, didn't look even when his mother screamed in pain and his father was begging for his life. Tears continued to fall down Barion's face and it took all his effort to stay quiet when he threw himself into a cave off the road. He heard the horses come running by, and heard the men ordered to search the woods. But he stayed quiet, even when the men walked by the cave and ignored it. He stayed quiet as he watched blood drip off their swords.

Barion wondered if his parent's lives had been worth his own. Ever since he had been born, he had cost them.

His mother told him that all the physicians she brought him to thought it was strange he grew so slow. After all, when he was five years old, he still only looked to be two years old. That was when his parents first moved, far away from Oakgrove. Every few years they had to move. Once they started getting questions on why their child was so smart when he was so young and why that child would glow occasionally, his parents had no choice.

One day, his parents were talking to a farmer and the farmer asked them how to best get a crop yield of wheat. Well, seven-year-old Barion thought the pair of oxen were very cute and decided to pet them. One glowing light later, Barion had the answer, and the farmer was out two oxen. That night, his parents had laughed with Barion about it over a bowl of beef stew. That had been the last carefree night. The next morning, Barion and his parents were running to a different town, far away from the farmer and his tales of a young boy who made a pair of oxen disappear.

Now Barion was on the run because of that gift. A gift that had cost him his parents.

Barion stayed there for a while before he left. Two nights had passed before he felt safe enough to leave the cave and he ventured into town. Without his parents, no one would recognize the boy. So, he stuck to young couples as if he was one of their children so no one would ask why he was alone. Barion tried asking himself questions- where his parents were, why he couldn't die, when he would die. He never got that glow, never got an answer. For two years, Barion was homeless. He stole bread from the baker, stole meat scraps from the butcher, and veggies from farmers.

He knew his parents had wanted him to go to the school in Corsair. They told him it was the only place he would be safe and the only school that could teach him about his magic. That was where they had been on the run to. His parents had died trying to get him there. But... This gift was the reason why his parents had died. It was more of a curse than anything. So, Barion had tried getting some sort of job in a tavern or selling newspapers. Anything. But when people looked at him, they saw a boy half his real age and didn't trust him. Sent him back off to his parents. And when they did that...

Barion moved from city to city. He hid in the carts of

merchants, which was easy enough to do at his size. So far, even if anyone did find him, they merely threw him out and told him to run back off to his parents.

But then Barion made a man's gold disappear one day, and he supposed he didn't have much of a choice but to run off to the school. It was either that, or the man would kill him. He still wasn't sure *why* the chest of gold had disappeared.

The man threw the bags out of the carriage while Barion stood there, quivering in his boots. "Where'd it go? Bring it back you street rat!" He screamed in Barion's face. Barion stood there shaking, not able to say a thing. "Bring it back!" The man pushed Barion to the ground, watching him.

Barion shook his head. "I don't know sir, honest. I can't bring it back because I didn't take it!" The man took a few steps forward as he pulled out a curved dagger. Barion threw his hands up and scrambled back. "Wait! I can answer any question. I'll do it for free." Barion had no idea if it would be free, but he hoped to the gods that the gold he made disappear would cover it.

"Who killed my mother?" The man growled out, clenching the grip of the curved dagger.

A faint golden glow appeared in Barion's palms as he delved for the answer and- *there.* "Your wife. She was irritated that your mother kept stopping by and thought your mother was trying to poison her. So, she poisoned your mother before your mother could poison her... But your mother just wanted to help around the house." The man's mouth fell open and his face grew red. Suddenly, Barion wondered if he shouldn't have answered.

"That lying bitch! I knew she was up to no good! Run before I decide to gut you like a fish." Barion knew that the man was telling the truth and ran like hell out of the woods. He ran down the paths and turned off the road if someone came by. When he finally got to the next town, he felt for the two pieces of gold left in his pocket and decided he had no tears left to cry.

After that, Barion decided he would go to that school, if only to figure out how to control his powers so he didn't have to use them. If he could control them, he could avoid ever using them. But when he got there, the god who oversaw the school had an ultimatum- he either accepted his powers or he found somewhere else to go. And for Barion, whose parents had died to get him here, that wasn't an option. Barion spent five years under the god's direct tutelage. He trusted no one else, and the god didn't blame him. In five years, Barion learned how to correctly use his powers and, more importantly, how to control them. The god did explain to him that the full extent had yet to be seen, but the older Barion got, the more he would learn.

Barion began taking clients to help him pay for his expensive moves. Some of them just didn't seem to understand that the rules weren't up to him.

"I don't know why we should pay you that much. Why can't you just tell us?" The man was badgering, throwing his hands up in the air. Barion tapped his fingers against the table impatiently.

"As I told you before, I may be able to find any truth, but the truth requires you to pay a price. It keeps the scales in balance. In some cases, the price has already been paid. In others, a payment or a greater payment still is required. You either pay or I cannot find the truth for you." Barion sat back in his chair, crossing his arms across his chest. "As I mentioned: if you want to know how to spin gold, you'll have to give me gold. I can't keep the gold, if you think I'm getting paid on top of what you already gave me. It goes to the gods who gave me my gift."

The man scoffed and walked out of the room, muttering something. Barion shook his head and slammed the door.

Insufferable cheapskates. If only they knew how reasonable his prices were. He wasn't the only truth seeker, but they were rare, and their prices were immense. Barion… Barion knew the true cost of this gift. He had no control over what the gods would require to balance the scales. That could only be discovered when the question had been asked. For his own price, Barion wanted to at least make the price to use his service in the first place affordable. If his clients could not pay what the gods demanded… That was their problem, not his.

He set the kettle over the fire and cozied up in his armchair. A salmon sizzled in a pan, and he watched it carefully. Through the open windows, a breeze blew through the room and he smiled, waving a little as if the god could see him.

Peace and quiet finally settled upon him. That was what he truly wanted. Visitors often came at all times of night, and it was rare he got a moment to himself.

A knock sounded at the door. "Oh, what do you want now?!" Barion growled as he took the salmon off the fire, setting the pan on a trivet on the table. He carefully pushed the asparagus over and cursed- the potatoes were cold by now. No use crying over cold potatoes, he told himself as he put the salmon on top of them. He drizzled a little of the oil over the potatoes and asparagus, hoping to warm them up a little. A knock sounded again at the door. "Oh, piss *off*!" Barion yelled. He had taken visitors all day- he hadn't eaten in hours, and he would be damned if he let this meal go to waste.

Then a small surge of power that even Barion couldn't ignore was flung through his house. He gulped, wondering if that breeze had been the god telling him he was coming, and if he had just told him to piss off.

Barion set the pan in his sink and tiptoed to the front door, looking out the peephole. Relief filled him- it wasn't the god, but two haggard travelers. They reminded him of his parents-a woman and man, torn cloaks, and panic in their eyes. He sighed and opened the door.

"My apologies, good sir and lady. You had just caught me right before dinner. Would you like to come in?" Barion wasn't stupid. He knew inviting them into his house was dangerous. Impulsive yes, stupid no. He was well aware of the trouble he was bringing upon himself.

The couple nodded eagerly, pushing back their hoods, and coming inside. Both looked familiar, but he couldn't place a finger on why. He had blond hair that reached his shoulders and she had white hair that reached down to her lower back. The man's eyes were as blue as the ocean and the women's eyes were black as night, with specks of silver throughout. Barion told himself that the sword at the man's side was purely for show. They took a seat at his table and Barion put his salmon off to the side. From the kettle he poured three cups of tea.

Three cups of tea that would have been for me, he thought with a frown on his face as he grabbed the honey.

"We were told we could find a truth seeker here. Is that true?" Barion nodded, letting the woman continue. "My husband- we believe he has an immortal soul. We need you to find the truth on if his immortal soul is there and if it can be released."

"That's bending the rules a little. Even if I could, the price would be great." Barion was already searching, though.

The man gave the woman a look, as if saying that they didn't have to do this. The woman just ignored him, focusing on Barion. "It's a price I'm willing to pay. I was told you were the best, and my witches do not lie. Can you help us, or not?"

Barion froze. Witches? What the *hell* was he getting himself into? "Who are you two?"

The woman smiled. "Who we are is of no concern to you. But those family trees over there will give you a hint. I didn't pin Makani as the regifting type- my witches won't be too pleased." As she spoke, Barion didn't even need to try to think if she was telling the truth. He felt it as surely as one felt like they were hungry or tired.

He eyed the family trees on the wall- Makani had given them to him as a present for graduation. Those were magical family trees of every kingdom in Tarlatan. Every time a member of the royal family was born, legitimate or not, they would appear on these family trees. There, at the bottom of the lines of Oakgrove and Rosenfall, was the man and woman.

Makani said it would help him ensure that he understood how the politics of the continent worked should he ever tangle himself with royals, but clearly that hadn't worked so well.

"I can do it- but to find an immortal soul, I'll need a piece of your own. It will feel like a piece of you is missing. You won't be any less immortal, but that part of your magic... That will be gone. I need something to help sniff out the soul and in doing so, you will have to sacrifice that part of your soul. My own cost..." Barion paused. "I will do it for free. Losing a piece of yourself will cost enough as it is."

The man stood abruptly. "Ravenna we-" She pushed his shoulder down with one hand and forced him to sit.

"Take it. I understand the cost." Ravenna cut off her husband and held out her hand. Musical notes floated above her hand, twirling around an orb of light. Barion looked her in the eyes for a second before he held out his own hand, letting part of her soul float over to his hand. A tear fell down Ravenna's face for just a moment before it fell off her cheek and onto the table.

He cupped the part of the soul in both his hands, cradling it to his chest as though it could break at any moment. The room was filled with golden light and song, a tendril of musical notes and light trailing towards the man's chest. In Barion's head, he saw the soul, a man pounding against an iron door. That man in the soul saw him and fell to his knees, pleading to be let out. Telling him that the coven could do it, but he needed to be out.

The light faded, settling back into Barion's hands. The musical notes were the last to wink out. "He does have an immortal soul- one locked away and desperate to be let out, it seems. Your coven will be able to release it, but it will take no small amount of magic."

The man was gripping the woman's hand and kissed her cheek. She stood on wobbly legs with the man bracing her. "Thank you, Barion. We have but one more favor to ask of you."

At this point, Barion's dinner was likely already frozen anyways. "What is it?" Screw it, curiosity got the better of him.

The woman stared him down with her black and silver speckled eyes. "Evil is coming. Evil that me and my husband alone cannot defeat. Promise me that when the time comes, you will come to the Ionian mountains and find us. We will need your help. Enjoy your dinner." Barion was on an impulsive streak tonight anyways, so he nodded. What could go wrong? They were likely full of shit anyways, he thought, and would never need him.

He walked them out the door, watched them walk down the path and hop onto their horses. He watched those horses until he couldn't see them anymore to make sure they were well and truly gone.

And then Barion ran back to the table, thoroughly starving. To his surprise, the food on the plate was steaming, with the salmon still sizzling a little and the potatoes as if they had just come out of the pot. Even the asparagus was perfectly warm, if not a little burnt. He looked back out the window as if he could still see the couple, raising an eyebrow.

As Barion scarfed it down, he thought back to before his parents had realized he was a different and before they had needed to run. Those ragged strangers had reminded him so much of his parents. The utter devotion and loyalty to each other, no matter the cost.

He poked at the potatoes. The night he had made those oxen disappear, after laughing with his parents, he had asked them what was wrong with him, and why they had to move so often. His mother only pulled him close and told him there was absolutely nothing wrong with him and that anyone who told him differently was just scared.

When his parents had been killed... Barion asked what was wrong with him, and no one was there to answer. No matter how many times he tried, he couldn't find the truth about himself. Perhaps the price was too great. But hadn't he already paid the ultimate price? Back then, he didn't even realize that finding the truth had a cost. He just knew that things occasionally disappeared when he touched them looking for the truth.

Now Barion tried to live in peace. He forgot about the ragged strangers who had come to his house and tried to find some sense of normalcy. It was the same routine day in and day out for thirty years. Every five years he packed up his house and moved to a new city in a different country. Visitors came and went, and his wealth grew. He used the money to build schools for orphans like he had once been, so that no one would have to suffer like he did. Sometimes he met folks that he sent to Makani.

Other times, people became too greedy.

"I'm telling you; I can't find the truth of when you will die. The future is hazy and constantly changing." Barion held his hands up, back against a wall. The man in front of him held a dagger to his throat.

"I'm the richest man in Oakgrove. You're telling me there is nothing I can pay you to sweeten the deal?" The man pressed the dagger harder into Barion's throat.

Then- that feeling in his chest. "You're going to die now." There was a faint glow, and then the dagger was released from his throat. The man's face was one of complete shock- Barion heard a knife slide out of the man's back and as he fell, a man stepped out from behind him.

He pressed harder against the wall. A soldier from the King of Corsair. A man whose king had ordered Barion to be found at any cost, including the life of innocents being taken.

"Ty, at your service." Ty sheathed his knife, holding out his hand. He shakily held out his own, shaking Ty's.

"Barion, at yours. Thank you for saving me. A stroke of luck I suppose!" Barion pushed himself off the wall, laughing nervously. Perhaps it was just a stroke of luck. The goons that had originally been following him ran in the opposite direction, so Barion at least could get home safe. Perhaps this soldier would be helpful.

"Not a stroke of luck, I'm afraid. When you entered the capital three days ago, the King tasked his guard to find you."

Barion froze. Utterly froze.

He had avoided Corsair for years after graduating from Makani's school because of this very reason. He moved around to different cities in different countries all for the hope that the King would have forgotten about him. There were other truth seekers in the world- why couldn't the King have hunted down them instead? In fact, the only reason Barion had entered Corsair was to work his way to Nazare. He couldn't have cut across the Center and going through the north would have taken far too long.

So Corsair it had been, and thus he had ended up in this situation.

"I think you have the wrong man, I'm afraid. Barion is a rather common name where I come from in the north…" Barion tried slipping past Ty, but he jumped in front of him and blocked his exit.

The next time he thought he'd take the short route to save

some time, he would remind himself of what happened when he did decide it would be worth it.

If there was a next time.

Ty held up his hands defensively, but Barion still took a step back, not trusting the man. "If King Tarrion wanted you dead, he would have ordered it already. He has no use for you, dead *or* miserable." Miserable? He had been miserable for years. Still was. King Tarrion had ordered the murder of his parents-there had been no other explanation for the lengths his soldiers had gone to. Ty gave him a pitying look, as if he somehow understood his situation. "Please just meet with him. He has given his word that you will be allowed to leave without any strings tied should you choose to."

Barion felt for the truth and a faint glow lingered between them before he nodded. The gold in his pocket clinked away as if it never existed.

Ty and Barion walked through the streets of Lubeck, the capital of Corsair. It wasn't the most beautiful city in the world, but was far better than the rest of the country. Half of it was deserts and the other half was grasslands and Lubeck lay right on the border of Corsair and Statium, where the lands turned into rich meadows with pockets of forests.

The vendors were merchants from the East, various types of fae and half breeds. It had become a trading hub to replace Luce Stellaraum for the merchants that still dared venture anywhere near it. Most stuck to the main ports in Tetanus, where the Canberran pirates offered protection. All that Corsair was left with was the remnants of a legacy they had not been prepared to take.

"My parents were murdered by highwaymen. It's why I became a soldier for the King in the first place. Corsair was not always my home, and it may not be the most beautiful place in the world... But my husband calls it home, and now the only family I have is here." Ty spoke softly, glancing at all the folks wandering through the streets. One hand was kept permanently on the pommel of his sword.

Barion watched the street children grab sweets off a stand and run as fast as they could, squealing in delight. The baker was yelling with his fist in the air and sat back down with his brows furrowed. He didn't bother responding, not even knowing what to say. What could Barion have done? Allied with another country who would have used him just like the King of Corsair?

He felt the sweat dripping down his back as the sun beat down on the city. Corsair was brutally hot in the spring. His parents told him stories of how Luce Stellarum had developed ways to cool down their cities during the hottest part of the day, but Corsair had never been wealthy enough to bring in their scholars to renovate their cities.

Barion and Ty walked through the gates of the looming sandstone castle, remnants of an ancient city far more powerful than any in existence today. King Tarrion touted that it was the summer home for the gods and historians argued that there was no proof of gods ever living there. But King Tarrion had cemented his rule as long as he was allowed to live in the summer palace of the gods, and his people were happy somehow. The main capital was no better- ancient, dilapidated homes barely kept up. From his experience, Corsair was far more pristine than Oakgrove- but they were the kingdom of light and morality and did not care for things of beauty.

Ty paused at the door to the main hall. "Are you ready?" Barion shrugged, looking back down the stairs and into the city.

"As ready as I'll ever be." Barion took a deep breath and walked into the room as guards opened the doors. It was an amphitheater styled room, with one main dais below the seating. There the King sat, his hands folded in his lap and a book on the lectern in front of him. The picture of... Calmness. As if he hadn't been chasing down Barion his entire life and this was the moment he had been waiting for.

Perhaps Barion was both impulsive and stupid, now that he thought about it.

The King's head glanced up, a smile on his face. He motioned the guards out and closed the book. "Hello, Barion. This day has been a long time coming. Please, take a seat." Barion sat across from King Tarrion, not quite pulling his chair in. He wanted the ability to make a hasty exit if he had to. "When I heard you were in the city, I ordered my best men to track you down. You've slipped my grasp quite a few times and I couldn't let you leave Lubeck without a chat first."

He paused, looking Barion up and down. Barion supposed he was looking for some sort of glow, but he wouldn't show any signs yet. He wanted this meeting to go on his terms.

"I suppose you set the goons on me in the alleyway, then?" Barion thought it was mighty coincidental that Ty had gotten there right before he was about to be killed.

The King, however, couldn't have looked more surprised. "Why would I set any goons on you? I ordered my men to bring you back unharmed and safe. I want your loyalty and trust."

So much for this meeting going on Barion's terms, then.

"And you thought you'd gain my loyalty and trust when your men killed my parents?"

King Tarrion's mouth fell and closed again like a fish out of water. "What do you mean?"

"Forty two years ago, my parents were murdered by soldiers of Corsair sent by orders from you, King Tarrion. You were a new king and wanted a truth seeker on your court. Corsair had only become weaker after Luce Stellarum fell, and you did not want your father's weak legacy on your side." Barion scoffed, voice growing quieter with each word. But any anger Barion held dissipated when King Tarrion leaned back in his seat and blinked a couple times.

"Barion... Barion, those were not my men. I ordered my men to find you and your family and bring you back alive. I wanted you to be happy here. That couldn't happen if your parents were dead." King Tarrion covered his mouth with his hand. "I can't believe they're dead."

Barion couldn't take this. He stood abruptly and pushed his chair back, taking a few staggering steps away. "I can't- I - I can't do this."

"Barion, I think you should stay. Someone impersonated my men and killed your parents. You know this is the truth. I'll pay the price, whatever it takes." Tarrion stood from his seat, walking to Barion. "You have to try. Please."

Barion didn't need to try, though. The book that Tarrion had just been reading disappeared and a faint glow appeared in front of Barion. A golden ball settled in hands that Barion held out in front of himself. It revealed a king mourning over his father, handing a letter off to guards.

Although he couldn't tell from the golden ball, Barion's soul knew what the letter said- and that King Tarrion was telling the truth. "If you weren't hunting me down, who was?" Barion let the golden ball float to the ground and looked over at Tarrion, who shrugged.

Barion's mind wandered back to those two strangers who entered his home all those years ago.

Evil is coming. Evil that me and my husband alone cannot defeat.

"My best guess?" Tarrion sat back down on his chair. "Whoever set Hallenfall ablaze and razed Averell to the ground."

CHAPTER 8

HEIR TO DARKNESS

HIS MASK TUGGED AT HIS EARS, BEGGING TO SLIP OFF. TENDRILS of light floated off of his costume, desperately wanting to search out the power that beat faintly in the distance. It called out to him, begging him to come. He wiped the thought from his mind, focusing instead on the ball. His friends- knights-surrounded him, laughing and pretending to drink. Most of this party was Rosenfall nobility, however. The drinks were just for taste- the people of this land were in tune with its magic and the alcohol had little effect on them. If his men didn't get a new goblet at least once, there would be suspicion.

He took a long drink out of his own goblet, savoring the honeyed wine. His magic bubbled, tendrils flaring out a little more. For the first time in his life, he felt free. At this party, in this land, his magic was not out of place. It could be on display, and no one would bat an eye.

Make it easier to blend in, his king had told him.

This wasn't just attending a costume ball in another nation.

He, as the Crown Prince of Oakgrove, was to use his power and defeat the Dark Queen of Rosenfall. Once she was defeated, his father's armies could march in and burn out the darkness.

Of course, no one had dared to ask for the prince's opinion. If they had, he would have told them it was a fool's errand and Rosenfall would not falter with or without their queen. But he was Kal, the Hero of Oakgrove, Heir of the Light, and Crown Prince of Oakgrove. He was not given an opinion.

"Kal, have you found her here?" His second in command spoke into his drink, eyes flitting around the room. Kal shook his head and snatched an hors d'oeuvre off a platter from a passing waiter.

His mouth watered at the rich spices and fresh vegetables that Rosenfall had. Oakgrove... Up in the mountains, sequestered away from major trade by years of war against Rosenfall, they had none of this. The priorities of his king were survival, not actually living. But here, in this place, surrounded by magic... He wondered how bad this could actually be... How bad enjoying their short lives could possibly be.

His second in command tapped his shoulder. "Kal, you in there? Guards are coming over. Could you dampen the light a little?" Serene calm was written across his second's face, but Kal saw the irritation in his eyes.

So, Kal begged the power inside him to dampen, tried to bury himself in it as to appease the magic and stamp it out. The Guards came closer, no smiles on their faces.

"Please hold out your hands. We've been told that spies from Oakgrove are here possessing stolen magic." Kal didn't need to look at his knights to know the deep shit they were in. Perhaps- perhaps once they tested his magic, he could convince them that his knights were to be trusted and didn't need to be tested.

He held out his hand, confident in his own magic, but despite that confidence in himself it still flared brightly.

Tendrils wrapped around him protectively, curling around his hands as the wand waved over them.

Something was wrong though- he felt it in his bones as the tendrils of light wrapped around his arms and hands fully now. The guards cocked their heads, smiling.

"Found a traitor on the first go. She will be happy that the traitor has been rooted out." The Guard met eyes with the others, who took out their wands. "Everyone, move!" The Guard shouted, light beaming out of his wand and directed at the floor behind him.

The most magical and terrifying moment of his life occurred right then- the guards had formed a circle, lights beaming out of their wands in unison with words they murmured silently. A breeze flew up behind him- no, *around him*. This breeze encompassed his knights and the Guards, forming a forcefield around them.

Kal would have laughed in joy and amusement, but he was in a room full of magic users, and he was the only one of his entourage that had magic. The crowd around him merely took a few steps away, as if nothing was happening.

As if spies from Oakgrove sent to kill their Queen were not in their midst.

"Can they hear us?" Kal's third in command spoke up suddenly and Kal turned to look at the grimace on his face. The Guards shook their heads. "Good. Let's just get this settled- I can't stand being in something so…" He crinkled his nose in disgust. "Unnatural."

Kal blinked. Blinked again. His third was so… Casual.

"Something the matter, Prince?" The Guard that had waved the wand over his hand spoke tauntingly, a smirk on his face. Kal wanted to wipe that arrogance off of it.

"Timren- ready on my command." Kal spoke, refusing to answer the question. His hands flared brightly again, his magic readying beneath his skin.

Timren, his second in command, stole his breath from his lungs. Timren ignored Kal, speaking to the Guard. "Kal isn't a prince anymore. He's going to be found dead outside Oakgrove, correct? You'll charm corpses to match ours, and we'll become wealthy landowners on the islands far from Rosenfall and Oakgrove." Kal choked a little.

"Timren?" His words were whispered out, not so strong as before. His second turned to him, no hint of sorrow on his face.

"We were never coming to kill the Queen. That was *your* mission. Our King gave us another- ensure you never came back from Rosenfall. Best case scenario, the Queen was here, and you killed her. Worst case scenario, this happens. I'd say I'm sorry but... I don't have it in me to lie. It's been exhausting having you so... so shiny all night." Timren waved his hand in dismissal of Kal and turned to the Guard. "That was the deal, correct?"

The Guard smiled, tossing a bag of coins to each of his five knights. "The Queen shall not forget this." His knights grabbed the money eagerly, stuffing it into their pockets. All around the forcefield, people continued on, as if they couldn't see what was happening.

His magic sang, screaming to be let out inside of him. The tendrils of light were still wrapping around him, desperately trying to protect him in the only way they could until he called upon his magic.

If he called upon his magic.

Perhaps it would be better to die here tonight- die a hero, rather than fight his way out and return to living a life of people hating him for his magic.

But his mother... She would never have let this happen. Why would his father give such an order?

"Timren, as your Crown Prince, I'm ordering you and the rest of my knights to stand down. I'm going to escort you back to Oakgrove where you'll all be charged with treason. Our King and his Queen would never give such an order. They would never let their Heir of Light fall." Kal forced his voice to steady. Forced his hands to still. Meanwhile, his second barked out a laugh. Deep inside him... He knew his words were not true. His mother and father would have sold him to the highest bidder if it brought Oakgrove wealth once more.

"Don't you understand it Kal? The King gave the orders because you are no longer his heir. The Queen was pregnant, before we left. She would not have her baby harmed by your magic. Yesterday we received word she had given birth to a healthy, mortal, non-magical baby boy. You are no longer Crown Prince." His second shook his head, laughing a little. As if he was frustrated it was taking this long for Kal to understand.

But... It couldn't be. His mother hadn't been pregnant. She would have called for him. She would have sent word to him. Instead... She...

Had locked herself away in her court, not allowing Kal into that part of the castle.

Kal fell to his knees, the tendrils of light pulling away from him. He reeled it all back in, consoling his aching soul with spools of light. He didn't stop the guards as they put shackles on his, neck and wrists. Didn't stand as they attempted to force him up by yanking the chains.

No, he wouldn't go any further. They'd end him here.

The Guard gave Timren a look, who just merely shrugged his shoulders. As if he could care less where it happened, and just wanted to go spend his new money.

So the Guard pulled out a sword, handed the chains off to other guards, and readied it against his neck above the shackle.

The Guard pulled the sword away and swung it with all his might, only to be blocked by a wall of light where the blade would have struck against his neck.

Kal winced, not expecting the magic to protect him. He begged it to stop. Begged for it to all end before-

That *song*.

It caused his magic to sing again.

One of the Guards was asking what was happening and why the magic wouldn't go away, but Kal didn't care. They tried to strike again, and the magic formed another shield.

Then, a guard cursed and turned to the Guard holding the sword at his neck yet again. "We've gotta do this quickly before she-"

The forcefield parted just enough for a lovely voice to answer and lighting to crackle against the floors. It skittered towards him, his tendrils of light rushing out to meet the magic. Curiosity filled his soul and Kal dared to turn his head.

The Dark Queen herself strutted through the forcefield, her broom flying next to her. His mouth went dry. Her white as moonlight hair was braided tightly back and her silver speckled black eyes crackled with electricity. A fiery crown sat firmly on her head.

"I've never known the kingdom of light to sacrifice one of their own. What do we have going on here?" Her voice flowed through the air like music, wrapping itself around his heart. He checked, double checked, triple checked- he couldn't taste metal in the air. The Dark Queen wasn't using her siren song on him, then. The guards around them still held their wands dumbly in the air, at a loss for words.

One dared to speak. "My Queen, we were under the impression you would be with the covens for the evening." She cocked her head, before throwing it back and laughing.

She stalked forward and grasped the guard's chin with her black painted nails. "Do you make it a habit to do things against my word when you are under the impression I will not be there? I believe I said the Prince of Oakgrove was never to be harmed should he cross into our lands." The forcefield around them shook as she grasped the guard's chin even harder, drawing blood.

A blast of dark energy poured out from her, throwing the forcefield down. The guards that still held him clenched his shoulders as if their life depended on it. The guests in the room fell silent within an instant, all drawing their attention towards the Queen.

"It seems we have a traitor in our midst. I'm disappointed. I let free trade reign, free the people, ensure the Assembly of Representatives gives their opinions before I pass laws and yet... Still, you ask for more. Have I not been a lenient ruler?" Her voice boomed across the room, shaking the chandeliers. She threw the guard to the ground, her flames burning his body into nothing more than ash before circling his knights and her remaining guards. "Kal, Prince of Oakgrove, correct?" She stopped walking, kneeling in front of him.

He nodded, his tendrils of light pulling him towards her. He felt the guards tighten their grip on him to no avail. She smiled at the tendrils, holding out her hand and letting them wrap around her fingers. She formed a small flame that the tendrils danced around. Wonder, joy- pure bliss- filled his soul in a way it never had before.

He wrenched his hand from behind his back, the light from the tendrils blinding the guards holding him. They stumbled back, cursing him. "They've never done that before." He reached his own hand out towards the fire, a small blue flame that danced with the tendrils of light. It didn't burn, but instead encased his hand in a comforting warmth.

"Because, Prince, you've never met anyone who holds the same amount of power as you. It's rare that anyone holds a fraction of the power we have." The Dark Queen stood, leaving Kal kneeling before her. She turned to his knights, whose eyes were wide. He could practically smell the disgust rolling off them. "Kal, these men are not my own, I believe. I could smell their mortal blood the moment it crossed into my lands from the Ionian Mountains in the North. It's only fitting that you hand out their punishment."

For a moment, Kal was going to say that he couldn't move too far from the chains that were still held by other guards, but the Queen burned the chains away. He stood next to the Queen, rage burning in his soul.

"I should steal the light from your soul for your crimes." Kal bit the words out, thinking back to his own mother who had wanted him gone. His tendrils reached out for them, wrapping themselves around each of his knight's legs. They traveled up each of the guard's bodies, making the knights paler by the minute.

A hand on his shoulder made the tendrils pause, almost look back at him to see what they should do. "Prince, I have a solution, if you'd hear me out." The room was still silent, though the Queen now whispered. She leaned into him, mouth next to his ear. "I sense the immortality in your soul. It was locked by the hatred of your family. I can unlock it if you'd wish. You could be capable of so much more. The decision is up to you." Kal was stunned and almost speechless.

He had always felt it inside of him, that deeper power banging against a door. It had screamed to be let out, but something had always made him pause. Kal turned his head to whisper in her own ear, her breath still trailing against his cheek. "And what would the price be?"

He felt the Queen stiffen beside him. "A price only I can pay. I will never use your freedom as a bartering chip." For a moment, he wanted to scoff. All his life, his freedom had been used as a bargaining chip. Why would she be any different?

But her magic, her soul so close to his own... He knew she was telling the truth. He felt her hands trail up him and knew the game they were playing. Let the room think she was using her siren's song on him, trying to seduce him. His tendrils moved around them; her own flame was burning in her chest, right where her heart was beating wildly. He slung his hand around her waist, letting it settle on the small of her back. He pulled her closer, his mouth on her ear.

"How do you propose we get out of here?"

"We need to get back to my covens. Legend has it, the last person who held a power similar to your own could go to other lands within an instant. I can let my lords know that I will return once we arrive. Think of where you want to go and wish for it as hard as you can. Follow my lead, wait for my signal." She bit his ear, trailing down to his neck. She bit and sucked, causing him to let out a genuine moan. His head rested against her cheek and before he spoke, he checked once more for the metal taste that accompanied nonphysical magic.

Nothing. Deep in his soul, he could feel she was telling the truth. Even the banging in his soul had quieted, as if it was waiting on bated breath.

He pushed her away, feeling blood trickle down his neck as she bit down a little harder. She cocked her head, flame wreathing her hand. Tendrils of light formed a shield on one, while others waited at his side. Mirth sparkled in both their eyes, as they got ready to put on a show.

Kal hoped she knew it wasn't true as he spoke the words. "I'd sooner turn to dust before letting a half breed siren bitch seduce me."

Seventy-Five Years Later

She walked down the path, no breeze in the air or clouds in the sky. Finals were almost finished and she was one step closer to getting her degree. Nothing could have ruined this day.

Except... Except for the asshole in front of her, flaunting his magic and how he was going to be the new dark lord after his father.

His pitiful excuse of magic, meanwhile, was throwing sparks in the air and creating fireworks that she could create when she was three. She snorted, walking around them and continuing on her way.

She had better things to do and would not let this bastard ruin her day.

But then he *had to whistle.* "Woah, sweetheart, where are you going? Come back here!" Irritation caused her to grind her teeth, but she kept walking and stomped down the magic. She bit on her lip, the iron tang flooding her senses.

She kept walking and sped up a little more. He whistled again- snapped his fingers. He snapped his fingers again, and sent one of those *stupid sparks* flying and it hit her right in the shoulder in the form of an arrow that exploded into little hearts.

Most girls probably would have blushed, fawned over him, proclaimed that no one had ever done that for them before. She stopped, gritted her teeth again. She glanced over her shoulder, noting the burn hole in her favorite shirt.

She might have let it go, but then he spoke to one of his friends again about how, when he was the dark lord, no one would ignore him.

"How could anyone ignore you when you're so gods damn annoying?" She ground out, still looking away from him. His friend *oooo*'d him and she could picture the idiots next to him, giving him a look wondering if he was going to let that go.

"Oh sweetheart, how will anyone ever pay any attention to you when you can't even take a compliment from your future dark lord?"

That was what broke her. What caused all control to snap inside of her.

Tendrils of darkness shot out and she turned, lifting a finger, and pushing one of his friends to the side. Another lift of the finger pushed the other friend to the side.

Her soul was singing, finally free. The control she had forced onto her magic was finally gone. She was finally free, and her magic almost controlled her. She lifted both hands, tendrils flying out to grab the *future dark lord* by the neck and drag him to her.

"I won't need a future dark lord to give me compliments." She ground out the words, the tendrils wrapping tighter around his neck. He tried clawing at them, but his fingers swiped through nothing but air.

She laughed, liking the feeling of this. Loving the feeling of her magic finally being used.

"What, future dark lord? Where is all that magic of yours? Go ahead. Try to claw your way out. I'm waiting." She picked a piece of lint off her shirt, flicking it away. Even looked away to inspect a bird on a tree but found that the future dark lord was still struggling. She peaked inside of her at the heart of her magic to see if his magic was even coming close to striking her away from him.

She let out a laugh, twirling in the sunshine that fell upon her. She was *free, her magic was free.* "Oh, future dark lord, how will you ever become a lord when you can't even escape my magic? Someone ought to ha-" She let out a shriek and the tendrils of darkness pulled away before tendrils of light could slash through them. She fell to the ground before her father, who gave her a disappointed look.

"All we asked was for you to get through college. Control your powers that long and, after that, we would begin to train you." Her father knelt before her, that disappointment replaced with gentle understanding.

"I'm sorry, father. I tried, but then, that impish mortal- he sent an arrow of sparks at me, and started calling me sweetheart, and called himself the future dark lord and... I couldn't control myself. My control snapped. I'm sorry." Her words tumbled out of her, and she stared at the ground. She had done well for so long. She had kept a tight lid on her magic, never letting any spill out. She lived as though she was mortal, not letting her magic become a crutch. But today that control had snapped.

"Oh, had to be saved by Daddy, eh? I knew I was close." That future dark lord behind her sneered, backing away a little. Brushing himself off. She looked at her father, raising an eyebrow.

He gave her a look that said he knew why she lost control and stood. Clouds filled in the sky, darkening and growing heavy with rain. Thunder boomed in the distance and lighting flickered across the sky.

He turned towards the mortal stalking up towards him. "What do you call yourself?"

The mortal, that future dark lord, looked around in confusion before settling in on her father. He could feel that as surely as she could feel it, but she had grown accustomed to that energy the ancient power held.

"Ah... The... The future dark lord." He muttered it out, still confused by the ancient power that had entered the world. Her father pinned him down to his spot with a stare, his tendrils of light floating around his hands as they always had. As her own always had. A sweet laugh filled the air and a smile bloomed on her face.

"You brought mother?" She let out a grin as her father shrugged his shoulders and nodded. Of course- mother was never far behind her father.

Her father chucked a little. "She wouldn't let me have all the fun." The future dark lord sputtered a little bit, confusion the only thing keeping him in place. He blinked a couple of times.

"What fun?!" If she was being honest, he had ground out those words with a surprising amount of steel. The future dark lord, forgetting his shaking legs, stalked up to her father and stared into his eyes. "Your daughter attacked me. Shouldn't you be punishing her already?"

Her eyebrows raised.

Well, this will certainly be interesting.

Feet landed softly next to her, and a hand gripped her shoulder softly. Electricity crackled against the ground, skittering towards her father.

Her mother, in that purring tone she always spoke in, chastised her father. "Dear, I told you to wait until I got here. You look like you've squeezed the life out of the poor, young mortal already." Her father turned around, giving her mother an exasperated expression. Her mother gave a look back that most men would have run from and turned to her, kissing her forehead. "Thalia, you aren't hurt, are you?" The words were soft, gentle.

The poor, mortal, future dark lord sputtered. "She just nearly choked the life out of me! Do something!"

Oh, Thalia almost pitied this boy.

Thalia's father had turned back to the boy, who was utterly lost. She felt her father's rage fill the air. "So... Future dark lord..." Tendrils of light floated towards the future dark lord, traveling up his body and landing on his shoulders. "Kneel to your queen."

"What queen? I will do no such thing! My father will hear of this treachery."

Any pity left in her ran far, far away. Darkness spread around her at the insolence this young mortal had. Beside her, her mother's flames sparked, and thunder cracked overhead again.

"Future dark lord, do you know what lands you reside in?" Silence. "You reside in Rosenfall, a land that has been ruled by its Lords for seventy-five years. The Queen left clear instructions that her throne was to be warmed, not stolen out from under her. Who rules these lands?" Her father's light still drifted in the young immortal's shoulders, who had the nerve to scoff.

"Rosenfall has been ruled by my father for seventy-five years when the Dark Queen died at the hands of the Oakgrove Prince. Both bodies were lost to magic." Even as the young immortal said it, that cockiness seemed to fade. As if he looked at the woman standing next to her, the black eyes speckled with silver, lightning skittering against the ground... Looked at the tendrils of light sitting on his shoulders... And settled on the crown of flames atop her mother's head.

"I said *kneel*." Her father may have seemed deathly calm, but she still felt that rage in the air. The tendrils of light on the young immortal's shoulders pushed him to the ground on his knees. His eyes were wide as another tendril wrapped its way around his mouth, preventing him from speaking. Her mother stalked up next to her father, slamming her broom on the ground next to him. Lighting skittered towards the future dark lord, running it's way up his body and fizzling into nothing.

Thalia took her place on the other side of her father, hoarfrost covering the ground with each step. A tiara of darkness and stars formed on her head and a dagger of ice slipped out of her sleeve and into her hand.

Her father knelt in front of the dark lord on one knee, staring him in the eyes. "Choose your next words very carefully." The tendrils loosened. For a moment, Thalia didn't think the mortal would dare to say anything. Not for the first time today, fear flashed in the boy's eyes.

"But... You died, fighting her. Your light and her flames burned both your bodies when your magic burned out. You were a hero, not a villain." The young mortal spoke each word carefully, not daring to even stutter. Her mother barked out that sweet, sweet laugh.

"Oh sweetheart, don't you know villains aren't born, but made?" Her mother ran her hand through her father's hair, smiling softly despite the power rolling off of her. "Kal was an immortal trapped within a mortal's body. His family feared him from the moment he was born. He was never loved. His family protected their reign by making him out as some hero, preventing the darkness from flooding into their kingdom with his light." Thalia's dark tendrils wrapped around her protectively. She had only ever heard this story once.

Her father, to his credit, was still deathly calm despite the cocky mortal in front of him. "My own mother wanted me dead. My father organized my supposed murder. Me and the Dark Queen... Used that to our advantage but assumed her lords would have been more loyal to the Queen who had let their lands thrive for centuries." Her father was quiet for a moment, before his tendrils lurched back around the boy's face and blocked his mouth again. "You will find your father and let him know that his Queen has come back for her throne—warmed, I might add. If his stench is anything more than lingering, he will find his dark soul burned from the inside out."

With a flash, her father had pulled in all his tendrils and pushed the young mortal to the ground. He scrambled up, running away from them as quickly as he could.

Thalia toed the ground. "So... I know it wasn't the grand entrance you meant for it to be..." She let the words trail off. She had been so close. So gods damned close to controlling her magic and mastering it...

Her mother's fiery crown flared a little before cooling into blue flames. She moved around her father and placed both hands on either side of Thalia's face. "Moonbeam... You are the product of something that should have never happened. Nothing has ever been the way it was meant to be and yet, I would change none of it for the world." Her father stood, standing behind her mother and placing his head on top of hers, not being burned by the flames.

Her heart stuttered a little, overcome by shame. "But I couldn't control my magic." She was almost ashamed to say it.

She had been asked to do one thing... And couldn't. Her father ruffled her hair and placed a hand on top of her mothers. She leaned into their hands, savoring the comfort.

"Thalia, if you are ashamed of that, then we have not raised you as we should have. When you are young, your magic is unpredictable. We wanted you to be able to grow in a world where you were not in danger. You have kept your magic practically under lock and key for twenty-six years. You are still young... We could not expect you to be able to control that much power yet." Her father paused. "Your mother's grandmother was a siren from the Northern Straits. She could control water and hoarfrost, but for years it would not listen to her. She would permanently moor ships in the ice, melt the ice around others, and freeze dinner. But she learned to control it. It took time. Control doesn't mean being a prisoner within your own body. You will figure it out in time."

Thalia nodded against their hands, but pulled away. "You didn't sing the siren's song. Why? You use it on Father when you get angry. Did you learn to control it?" Thalia looked into her mother's eyes and found nothing left of the evil that had filled them before. Instead, sadness and love clouded them.

A tear rolled down her mother's face. "Thalia... That song, it has no power. I gave it up to free your father's soul from his mortal body. Your father simply can't say no when I sing that song because I have him wrapped around my finger." Despite the tears, her mother chuckled, Thalia and her father joining in.

Thunder cracked overhead with tendrils of light and darkness wrapping around the three. A wave of power blasted out from them, announcing their arrival.

The Dark Queen, the Heir of Light, and the Heir of Darkness had come for their thrones.

Timeline

1539 — Kal and his knights attend the ball in Rosenfall

1565 — Natalia is charged with murder

Statium burns to the ground

Luce Stellarum is attacked and falls

1574 — Thermaxas meets Jonathon

1575 — Seeker of Corsair attends Makani's school for five years

1585 — Kal and the Dark Queen approach the Seeker of Corsair

1614 — Natalia faces a threat Remy has not seen in many years.

Princess of Fire and Ice comes into her power as The Dark Queen, Kal, and Thalia reveal their power

Sentinel finds Thermaxas through Jonathon

Analise receives word that she is to bring her armada to the Ionian Mountains